City

City of Allegory

The Immanuel City Saga

A Novel by Brady Goodwin, Jr.

To Chad Horton, as you play your role in the mission + movement, I pray that God will satisfy your appetite and show you the place of this offering, as we eagerly await to sit at his table again.

Brady Jackson

1/2012

Self-Published through UrbanRemixProject.com

City of Allegory: The Immanuel City Saga

Copyright © 2011 Brady Goodwin, Jr.

Self-Published by Brady Goodwin through
Urbanremixproject.com

Philadelphia, PA

Printed in the United States of America by Createspace

Cover art and sketch: Reggie Byers;
www.reginaldbyers.com

ISBN-10: 0615559956
ISBN-13: 978-0-615-55995-7

I take no delight in corruptible food or in the dainties of this life. What I want is God's bread.

–Ignatius (circa) 110 A.D.

Contents

Episodes

Prologue

Khalil sat at the long, lavish banquet table thinking about everything he had just survived and how close he had come to meeting disaster: almost freezing to death, being thrown into the great fire that burns continually, being torn apart by the lions, losing his family, gaining his family, being consumed by the light that transformed the city; it was almost too much. But then, it dawned on him that every single person sitting with him around that unending table had a story of how they came to be there.

He wondered if he would get to hear about their adventures and learn how all of their experiences tied together. But there was one story he wanted to hear more than the rest—the story of the man sitting across from him—the one they called Tru-man. Their lives were intimately connected. But, while Tru-man knew all about Khalil, Khalil had not yet heard Tru-man's whole story, the story which you are about to read. However, this book is not about Tru-man or Khalil. This is the incredible saga unveiling how they came to have their souls fed and filled in a nameless city, while seated at the table from the great hill.

Soul Fooled

"Yo, I'm starving!" Trumaine screamed. Word had been spreading around town about a bangin' soul food restaurant not too far outside the city. There was only one problem: it was located where very few people had the courage to go. Trumaine called out, "Anybody down to go to that soul food spot up in the hills?" But no one answered, so he continued working. The chains dangling from his neck down to his wrist kept getting tangled up in his work. By noon, he was just as tired from constantly untangling his chains as he was from doing his actual job.

He had learned not to mind them too much though. Everyone he knew had the same chains connecting both of their hands to their neck and, some people's chains were actually quite stylish. Trumaine did not know how people got those trendy chains, but he hoped to be able to have that kind someday. Until then, he would not be able to take his rusty chains off, even if he wanted to.

Now, you're probably thinking, 'hands chained to his neck? What kind of place is this?' I'll tell you. Trumaine lived in a city like any other. And yet, his city was like none other. The city had no name, or rather, it was called Nameless City. Everything in the city was solar powered and if you were to visit, you would find many familiar features: stores, homes, restaurants, government officials, arts and entertainment with famous singers, rappers, athletes and actors, and people from various ethnic groups.

However, there were other features, such as the chains and a few other oddities which you will soon discover, that may not seem as familiar. But if you knew any better, you would quickly come to suspect that everything in this city was only a secondary reality; a mere symbol pointing to some higher, primary truth located somewhere else. Yet, most people here didn't know any better and so, their reality, as odd as it may sound to you, made perfect sense to them. But from time to time, that higher, primary truth would make its way down into the city to those who developed an appetite for it. And as you have just read, Trumaine was starving.

At about a quarter to one, his hunger pains returned and would not be ignored. He began to beg, "Please y'all, I've never been this hungry before. I'm tryna get that good soul food folks be talkin' about. I know somebody in here is feelin' me on this. Let's go up the hill." One of his co-workers pulled him to the side and offered, "Hey man, you don't think all of us are hungry too? Look here, I've got a ton of junk food in my locker. That should hold you, alright?" But Trumaine replied, "Nah man! That's not gonna cut it."

His co-worker complained, "Dag Tru-man!" (This was Trumaine's nickname.) "Just wait 'til after work and we'll go to the Halfway's-house and get some fast food." But Tru-man was no longer interested in these substitutions. His co-worker's voice got lower, "Okay listen. Maybe you don't know, so I'll tell you. But you're on your own after this." He turned Tru-man around and pointed to the top of the hill at the end of the busy street on which they worked. "You see that hill? Somewhere up there is supposed to be *THE* best soul food spot anyone here has ever heard of. But trust me, you don't wanna go there. Okay?" Unable to accept this, Tru-man demanded to know, "And why not?" The answer he received excited and frightened him at the same time. "Everyone who goes there either comes back completely different than when they left . . ." Before he could finish his thought, another co-worker named Jermaine jumped in with, "Or they don't come back at all."

Tru-man was curious. He inquired, "What do you mean 'completely different?'" The first co-worker began to explain, "Well, before people go there, they're just like the rest of us. They talk about the stuff we like talking about, they do the stuff we like doing. They're . . . you know, regular. But once they come back from there, if they come back at all, all they seem to wanna talk about is the soul food they ate there. I mean, I'm sure the food is good and all, but it can't be *THAT* good." After hearing this, Tru-man was determined to see for himself. He could not imagine anything tasting so good but, if such a thing existed, he needed to find out.

And so, he left his work station and headed to the locker room to prepare for his trip up the hill. It took him quite a while to change because of his chains, but no longer than usual. While he was getting dressed, Jermaine entered the locker room with a concerned look on his face. He stood, shaking his head slowly from side to side. Tru-man asked, "What's wrong Maine?" Jermaine replied, "He's not telling you everything about what happens to people who go up that hill." "Okay," Tru-man replied, "then why don't you tell me."

Jermaine began. "I'm sure you've noticed that there are some people in this city who have one hand completely free from any chains, but have you ever noticed that those are the same people who are always walking around singing the praises of that hilltop soul food spot?" Tru-man blurted out, "You know, I thought I noticed that but I wasn't sure." Jermaine continued, "All of those people used to have both their hands chained like us, but when they come back down the hill, their right hand is free and stays free for the rest of their lives." "Is that all?" Tru-man asked. "No," Jermaine shot back. "Some people come back down the hill with a lot of money. But they don't talk about the restaurant or the food at all. In fact, they come back hungrier than when they left. The chains binding their hands to their neck are more extravagant and flashy, but also much heavier than before, and harder to live with. They spend all their money trying to make their chains lighter again."

"Go on," Tru-man encouraged. Jermaine continued, "You know the people we see running around trying to get away from imaginary lions or something they think is chasing them? The ones who, when you try to talk to them, keep looking at their hands as if something was on them? All of that comes from that hill. They never talk about eating at the restaurant either. And then, there are those who come back and can't stop talking about a beautiful woman or some attractive guy they fell in love with up there. They're heartbroken and can't stop thinking about it. But they never talk about having had any kind of soul food.

"Now, I've heard that you're allowed as many trips up the hill as it takes to make it to the restaurant, but once you've eaten there you can never go back. They say you never need to go back; like the food sticks with you, like forever." "What?" Tru-man shouted out in disbelief. Jermaine shook his head and laughed, "I'm telling you Tru-man, there's something crazy going on up there. Nobody comes back acting right."

Tru-man thought for a second about those seemingly deranged people he had seen around town, running from invisible beasts. He did not want to become one of them. After hearing Jermaine talk about the different ways people return from the hill, he figured he had a one in four chance of coming back with his hunger satisfied and his right hand completely free from any chains. The odds were not in his favor but, just then, his stomach began growling louder than his inner thoughts. He knew he had to at least try to find this soul food restaurant. He told Jermaine, "Look man, this is *Me* you're talking to. I aint coming back no different than you see me right now. You feel me? Except I might have a lil' gut the next time you put eyes on me. Ya dig?" The two of them laughed and shook hands, and then, Tru-man closed his locker and headed for the exit.

He strolled down the street, thinking to himself that a 25% chance of success was not so bad. As he got closer to the bottom of the hill, familiar faces greeted him with strange looks. "Why are you going that way?" many asked. "You're not about to go up that hill are you?" others questioned. A few, realizing that he was determined to make the unpopular decision, began sending messages to people they knew saying, *"Get ready to say good-bye to Tru-man, he's going up that hill."* Others began stuffing all sorts of junk food into his pockets and backpack, "this is for when you get hungry, cuz you *WILL* get hungry," they laughed.

Tru-man thought about his family and friends, particularly, his brother and sister, and his ex-girlfriend with whom he still kept in touch. He wondered how they would treat him if he happened to come back from the restaurant changed in one of the four ways described by Jermaine. He came to the bottom of the hill and was tempted to look back down the long street leading to his job, to his friends. But he did not. He thought that if he looked back, he might be tempted to go back. And so, one foot in front of the other, up the hill he went.

He had not been walking for long when he came to a gate with a sign that said "Chain Exchange." He wondered if this was the place where the 25% lose or, at least, began to loosen the chain on their right hand. There at the gate stood a tall guard with a huge skeleton key. The guard informed him, "No chains on the hill beyond this point. Please pull down your shirt collar and expose your neck." Tru-man did what he was asked to do. The guard unlocked the iron collar around Tru-man's neck. He felt the enormous weight lifted from his shoulders and began to swivel his head around, all the way left and then all the way back to the right, enjoying the freedom. "Please hold out your hands," the guard requested. When Tru-man lifted his arms, he was startled by the graphic images of two lions, one tattooed on each of his hands. The one on his right hand was twice as large as the tattoo on his left hand. But where had these images come from, Tru-man wondered. Then, the tall guard at the gate mumbled something that sounded like, "Newman will explain it; if you make it that far." The guard unlocked his wrists and for the first time in over a decade, Tru-man was able to stretch and feel the full extension of his arm span.

The guard took Tru-man's chains and dropped them into a huge tray attached to a large scale. He then announced, "You have twenty-seven hours to make it to the restaurant at the top of the hill and return here with your receipt." Tru-man looked at the scale and saw that the weight of his chains was exactly twenty-seven pounds. The guard added, "If you do not return with proof to validate that you've been to the restaurant within twenty-seven hours, and you're still on the hill, you will be considered trespassing. You will be arrested; all of your chains will be reapplied to your neck and wrists and you will be forcefully deposited back into the city below. Do you understand these terms?" "I think so," Tru-man replied, "But which way do I go?" The guard looked at Tru-man as if he wanted to smile, but he did not. "Up," he said. "You go straight up, sir."

Tru-man walked past the gate and continued on for close to an hour. As the day went on, he began thinking, "I must be crazy to do all this just for some soul food." He thought this especially because he had never tasted this food before. What if it was not as good as he had heard? How foolish he would feel. But just as he was tempted to turn around, a gust of wind swept down upon him and brought the sweetest aroma to his nostrils. The aroma itself almost satisfied his hunger, even as it made him more eager to reach the top of the hill to have the actual food that produced the savory scent. He walked forward faster then, traveling happily for a while until, it began to rain. The sweet smell coming from the top of the hill was no longer in the air and his journey seemed all of a sudden harder and more unreasonable.

Was the fast food and junk food back home really so bad that he needed to go through all of this just to be filled? Come to think of it, he had some junk food in his pockets and even more in his backpack. Couldn't he just eat that and spoil any appetite he had for soul food? He walked slower now as he considered this option. Eventually, the rain stopped and he began to wonder if he had traveled too far to turn back. How would his friends look at him if he cut his journey short and returned home? Regardless, cancelling his travel plans seemed like the best thing to do. But he still needed to satisfy his hunger, even if it would only be a temporary satisfaction. He reached into his pockets and fished around for some junk food and pulled out a piece. Then, he stood for a while, looking down at the junk in his hands and again back up toward the top of the hill.

Just as he started to unwrap the unwholesome treat, he began to see shapes of what looked like groups of people coming toward him, making their way down the hill as he traversed up. As they got closer, he recognized some of these happy faces, though he had never seen them look this happy before. He knew some of them from the city but hadn't seen them for quite some time. "How are you?" he asked. "Have you been to the restaurant? Tell me how it was." Then, each one of them spoke from his or her own experience and talked about every detail of the restaurant: the host, the waiters, the chef, the menu, the food and edible eating utensils, the prices, the payment, the ambiance, the entertainment, the dress code, the clothes they were given to meet the dress code, and the one named Newman who sat at the head of the table, and on and on they went.

As they spoke, Tru-man remembered the words of his co-worker, "Once they come back . . . all they seem to wanna talk about is the food they ate there." And although this appeared to be true, as he listened to them talk with such joy and in such detail, he could not see how this was such a bad thing at all. Their words lifted his spirit and sped him on in his mission to have the same food and experiences they spoke of. One of them pulled out a menu to give to him and then, they all watched as he had the same strange experience each of them had enjoyed on their journey. As Tru-man glanced over the menu, he felt his appetite both quenched and deepened at the same time. It was almost like what happened earlier when the gust of wind enticed him, but this was much stronger. He felt as if he could end his journey right then and there, but also, that he must continue to climb. He began to shake their hands and hug them as he bid them fair well. He ran on up the hill from that point forward until he could run no more.

It was beginning to get dark and he wondered if he could make it up the hill before it got too late. He began to size up every group of rocks or trees he passed, looking to see if they would make a good shelter for the night. As he considered making camp, he was startled by two men who came rushing down the hill toward him. Tru-man got excited thinking, "Maybe they'll have more incredible stories about the great soul food at the top of the hill." But the two men did not have the same look of joy or contentment possessed by the first group he encountered. In fact, they hardly acknowledged him except for when they shouted, "Lions! Run!" Tru'man stopped and looked around. He stood very still and listened for the sound of the pursuing jungle cats but he neither saw nor heard anything. He shouted back at the men, "How was the food?" hoping to get some encouragement from their words. But they did not respond.

He did not know what to make of this, at first, but then he remembered Jermaine's words. Had he just passed those deranged souls who will spend the rest of their lives running from imaginary beasts? But, he thought, what if there really were lions on the prowl looking for someone to devour? Just in case, he did not want to fall asleep or let down his guard. Tru-man decided that he would not make camp but that he would continue walking. He made it to about halfway up the hill when he began to smell again the aroma of soul food. It was not as strong or as pleasant as the scent from earlier. Tru-man thought this was strange since he was now closer to the source than he was before. As he drew nearer, he saw a restaurant sitting just off the side of the road. Perhaps this was it, except, several things gave him reason to pause.

First, was the fact that the sign outside seemed to be spelled embarrassingly wrong. It read "SOUL FOOLED." He thought to himself that even if this is not the right place, still, he must go in to inform them of the incorrect spelling. But there was one other problem; to the far left and far right side of the building sat two large, leashed lions with long linked iron chains. Tru-man had always been very smart and athletic. If only he knew how long the lions' chains were, he thought, he could figure out a way to get to the door before they reached him. But, fear and common sense stopped him. He looked up toward the top of the hill, then back down at the entrance to SOUL FOOLED, and then back to the top of the hill. He thought to himself, "Did they mean for me to travel *ALL* the way to the top, or did they just mean that the restaurant was *TOWARDS* the top. Maybe this is the right place." But he considered that the joyful bunch of travelers he first ran into did not mention anything about lions. Only the second group of dissatisfied souls regarded these frightening beasts. He started to turn back to the road when, suddenly, someone appeared in the doorway and called out to him.

"Hungry?" The stranger shouted. "This is probably the place you're looking for. We have the best food on the whole hill. People come from miles away to eat here. Don't worry about these lions. Run if you like, or walk. They're on strong leashes. Each one can only get within six feet of the path to this door. They're just here for my protection." This gave

Tru-man some comfort and a little courage; six feet on both sides was a lot of room. He turned off of the road and onto the path of the restaurant, encouraging himself with the thought that behind those doors was the answer to his severe hunger. With that in mind, he ran toward the doors, even as the lions jumped up and ran toward him. Tru-man slowed down and stopped until he saw that the lions could not reach him. And indeed, they came close but could not get close enough. Not willing to trust the strength of the chains to hold them, Tru-man hurried up the steps.

He passed the beasts and laughed a fear-filled laugh of relief as he entered the restaurant. Inside, he saw pictures of all types of delicious dishes hanging on the wall. Yet, there were no other customers inside. Tru-man was guided to his seat and handed a menu. While looking over the list of options, he noticed that it neither satisfied nor deepened his appetite like before. He pulled out the menu handed to him by the traveler on the road and compared the two, only to realize that they were not from the same place. Feeling foolish for having gotten off the right path, he immediately got up and ran through the doors, past the lions and back to the road.

He began to get on with his journey when a voice called to him from the SOUL FOOLED restaurant, "Wait! Don't go! You're gonna miss the raffle. You're gonna miss out on the great food, and the raffle." Tru-man shouted back, "I'm sorry, I don't think this is the place I was looking for." He then added, "And, what raffle?" He slowed his pace just enough to hear the answer. The stranger shouted, "We have a raffle every day around this time, and since you're the only customer, you're almost certain to win." This was intriguing, but it would take a little more for him to be completely persuaded to return.

"What's today's prize?" Tru-man asked. The one calling to him, who owned the restaurant replied, "As much cash as you can carry out of here." This was always enticing to young travelers like Tru-man, especially since he had taken half a day off of work and was likely to miss work the next day as he returned from his soul food seeking adventure. Tru'man jogged back up to the door, challenging himself to be alert but not afraid of the charging lions. He was alert, and he was not afraid. However, he noticed that the lions seemed larger, or at least closer to him, this time around. But maybe it was all in his head.

Even more than the lions, his extreme hunger was gnawing at him. And so, the young traveler entered the restaurant to finally have his meal. He pulled a raffle ticket and to his delight, he won. The owner informed him that, after his meal, he would be allowed to go to the "cash and carry" room to grab as much money as he could. Tru-man thought about how much money he would be able to scoop up, especially now that his hands were not chained. He tested his arm span again and practiced the techniques he would use to collect the cash. But as he made the motions, he remembered the words of his co-worker Jermaine, "Some people come back down the hill with a lot of money to flash. But they don't talk about the restaurant or the food."

He sat for a while, thinking about this and waiting for someone to come take his order, but no one ever came. Another hour passed with no waitress attending, so Tru-man stormed into the kitchen. To his surprise, no one was there. He went next to the door of the back office and was about to knock but stopped when he heard two people talking. The conversation sent a combination of fear and rage surging through his soul.

1st Voice: Do you remember what to do?

2nd Voice: Yes, I watched you do it the first time after he came in, and again after he left; then again after he came back in. As soon as the customer gets tired of waiting to order and leaves, I'll run to each of the lions and add another one-foot link to their chains. Then go to the door and persuade the customer to come back in.

1st Voice: Okay, but he may have already noticed that the lions have been getting closer. And when he leaves this time, he will definitely notice. What will you say if he won't come back because of this?

2nd Voice: I will convince him that it is all in his mind; that his hunger is getting to him and that the chains are now the same length as before, so he is completely safe.

Tru-man could not believe his ears. He wanted to go in and confront them but did not know what might happen if he did. He turned instead and made his way to the door, building up his speed to get past the lions. Tru-man had always been very smart and athletic. Having done the math in his head, he figured the lions were now just three feet away from being able to reach him on the path. Seeing that one lion was larger than the other, Tru-man angled himself to go more towards the smaller lion in order to get a few extra inches of safety. As he leapt into the air, so did the huge, hungry cats. Tru-man smiled, taking pride in the fact that he was out-thinking and outmaneuvering those who tried to deceive him. His departing footsteps alerted the owner and his employee, who quickly got up and rushed to put the plan into action. By the time the employee got to the door, Tru-man was nearly back to the road, training his eyes to find and focus on the top of the hill.

But, just as he located and locked his sights on his target, he heard the most beautiful voice calling to him, pleading for him to return to the restaurant, "Sir, sir . . . Trumaine; aren't you hungry?" He stopped in his tracks and turned back to see who this beautiful voice belonged to. How delighted he was to see that the voice was just as beautiful as the lips that spoke the words. And the lips, just as beautiful as the face on which they were situated. He could not take his eyes off of her as she spoke, "Please forgive us for taking so long to take your order. If you come back in, I promise, you can have anything you want; even if what you *really* want is not on the menu."

Tru-man was enticed by her offer. But he remembered the conversation he overheard coming from the back office of the SOUL FOOLED restaurant. He inquired of her, "I heard two men talking about adding more links to the lions' chains. Aren't you working with them? Why are you trying to get me to come back in when you know the lions will be able to reach me?" "Sir," she replied. "I'll be honest with you. You're right. I work for the owner of this establishment. He lives to take business away from the soul food restaurant at the top of the hill. But he doesn't know how to make any of the food you see on our menu. And instead of feeding customers, he tricks them and feeds them to these two lions you see here. And I myself can only eat and get paid after the lions have been fed."

Tru-man was curious as to why she was helping the owner. He begged her to leave the restaurant and join him on his journey to the top of the hill. The employee seemed genuinely excited that he wanted her to join him, but she asked for one favor first. "Sir, please, the owner owes me a lot of money and will only pay me once he sees that you have come back into the restaurant. If you come back in one last time, I can get my paycheck and then I will show you how to exit through the back. No one knows this but, on the other side of this restaurant is the entrance to the underground mall that sits deep beneath your city. I'm sure you've heard rumors about it. Some of the employees here use it to enter into your city at night. We can use that to get you back home. And if you rescue me from here, I will stay with you. You'll be back in the city with no chains on your wrists and neck. And you'll have me!"

Tru-man had heard the rumors about the underground mall. But this was the first time he had heard anyone talk about an entrance to it. He was tempted to help her; the more he listened and looked upon her beauty, he felt himself falling in love. But his fear was too great. He asked, "What about the lions, their chains are longer now aren't they?" But her response convinced him that she was trustworthy. "Yes," she said, "but there's something else you need to know. When you first arrived, the owner told you that the lion's chains would stop them six feet short of the path. But he was lying. Their chains were really only five feet short of the path. He has added three links and, after you left the last time, I added another one, which makes them four feet closer to you than when you first arrived. But they are still one foot away from you on either side. If you stay right in the middle, halfway between them, you can make it. Once you come in and sit down, I will add another link and the owner will be expecting your body to feed his lions the next time you exit. But we will trick him and escape out the back. Then I'll travel with you to your city or, maybe to the top of the hill so I can finally have the soul food that I could never have while I was here."

Her beauty and logic captured his will. He would be one foot away from certain death on either side, but he had faith in his own intellect and athletic ability which had served him well in every other case. He motioned for her to move back in order to give him room to land. He then began to angle himself so that he could run and leap up the stairs at the end of the pathway. It all seemed to be happening in slow motion. He started to run, but so did the lions toward him. He began to leap, and so did the lions at him. But he noticed something eerily strange. The beautiful employee began to grin a very grotesque grin. While in midair, he thought to himself that once he landed safely, he would have to ask her what it was that was so amusing. But before he could land, he felt something odd. It was as if he was being suddenly and quite violently snatched backwards by his shirt collar. He ended up on the ground being dragged back to the road which leads to the hill top.

"Noooooo!!!!" Tru-man screamed. "What are you doing? Let me go!" But the one dragging him hurried all the more, explaining between desperate breaths, "I'm rescuing you. That's not the place you want to be. Those lions would have torn you to pieces." But Tru-man fought him hard, twisting and turning, kicking and clawing at the ground, "No, you fool! We had it all worked out. She was going to sneak me out the back door. We were going to travel together to the top of the hill." The one dragging him continued to take him back to the road. Once there, he blocked the way back to the SOUL FOOLED restaurant. Tru-man continued to attempt to go back in order to rescue the beautiful employee, but the one preventing him began to warn, "She is beautiful. But you should know that she is not just the owner's employee, she is his daughter." At that point, Tru-man began to calm down, somewhat. The rescuer continued, "And she is not just his daughter, she is also his son." Tru-man finally stopped and looked at the unsung hero as if to demand further explanation.

The heroic rescuer explained, "She becomes whatever the owner needs for his plans to work at any given time. I know these things because the owner of that deadly diner was once an employee of mine." "Who are you?" Tru-man asked. He looked at the man and then saw a name tattooed on his arm circling his bicep and triceps. Tru-man wasn't sure why, but the name meant something to him. Perhaps he had heard the name growing up in the city, he thought. In all the excitement, Tru-man forgot that this name had been mentioned to him twice already on his journey. "I'm Newman," the man said. "I'm the son of the owner of the soul food restaurant at the top of the hill. This place here only exists to steal my father's customers and keep people from tasting what we have prepared for them."

Newman saw that Tru-man was still thinking of returning to collect the beautiful employee or, turning to head back down the hill, ending his quest to be fed and finally filled. He said to Tru-man, "You can go back to the city, but you will go back hungry and heartbroken. And if you want to go rescue the beautiful employee, there's something that you should know. The owner of that place lied to you about the length of the chains around the necks of Curse and Consequence, the two lions guarding that place."

"I know," Tru-man interrupted, "she already told me, the chains were really five feet short at first." But Newman shouted to get his attention, "NO! The beautiful employee also lied. The chains holding back Curse and Consequence were only four feet short of the path to begin with. But between her and the owner, they eventually added back the missing four feet. It was her job to entice you to return one last time in order that those beasts could be filled while your hungry soul died to feed them."

Tru-man stood motionless as he considered the evil involved in the plot against him. He finally realized that none of his intellectual or physical abilities would have saved him since, the entire time, he was using them upon the landscape of an elaborate lie. He looked back at the SOUL FOOLED restaurant and saw the beautiful employee standing at the door being yelled at by the owner. He could not hear what they were saying. Maybe she really did want to leave with him, he thought. He was tempted to ask Newman why it is that he should believe him; but he stopped first to study his rescuer and noticed many half healed scars on Newman's arms and chest. Before he could ask why he was so wounded, Newman offered, "Walk with me, and I'll tell you how I got these." He put his arm around Tru-man and helped him turn away from the SOUL FOOLED restaurant. As they walked, Newman began telling the most fantastic story about the city below, the underground mall, the meaning of the chains, the first customers he ever had at his restaurant and so many other things as they traveled up the long road leading to the top of the hill.

Tru-man listened carefully. He wondered why he had never heard these things before. He planned to write about them and his experience at Newman and his father's restaurant at the top of the hill. And in fact, the time would come when he would do just that. But how could he have known the painful circumstances ahead which would actually cause him to write, or the high price he would have to pay in order to pass his pages along to those who would read his words, long after his pen would be laid to rest? He couldn't know. But thankfully, Newman did.

Episode TWO

Dinner with Friends

It had been a full twenty-four hours when Tru-man returned from Newman and his father's restaurant. With three hours left to spare on the hill, he passed the time with several friends he met while dining at Newman's table. As he and his new friends got close to the city, they came again to the Chain Exchange gate. The tall guard met them and demanded proof that they had indeed been to the restaurant at the very top. Tru-man pulled out his receipt with Newman's signature and presented it to the guard who scanned it with a handheld device.

Knowing what to expect, Tru-man moved his shirt collar out of the way, baring his neck, and waited. "Please pull down your shirt col . . ." the guard began to say but stopped when he saw that Tru-man had beaten him to it. The guard smiled a half smile and placed the iron collar back on Tru-man's neck. He then pulled out the lighter one of the two chains he had previously taken off of Tru-man the first time they met. "Congratulations," he said. "Looks like you're free from your heaviest chain." Tru-man smiled and replied, "Yeah, thanks to Newman." He waited for his friends on the other side of the gate as they each went through a similar process with the guard.

As soon as Tru-man and his friends got back into the city, all of their communication devices began buzzing and beeping with numerous alerts. They had been so focused on their journey and caught up in conversation the whole way back that none of them even realized that they were unable to receive electronic messages while on the hill. Tru-man grabbed his instant thought device or "connecter" (as they were called) and began to send thoughts like the following:

Guess what y'all. I finally ATE! No, I don't think y'all understand me. For the first time in my life I feel like I really ate. You might think you've eaten before, but I just came back from up the hill. I don't know what you've heard, but get at me and I will tell you what you've been missing— Tru'.

He must have sent about 1600 instant thoughts. He had over 2000 dots in his connector (every personal contact someone made appeared as a dot inside the device) so he created group-lists and different types of messages for different groups of friends, family and acquaintances. He wanted to set up meetings to tell them all about his hilltop adventure. Tru-man had never sent so many messages in one day before so he figured that was probably the reason for what happened next.

He received an instant thought message from his ex-girlfriend Kakei who asked, "*Is there really an underground mall that's still full of brand new merchandise?*" He attempted to respond with, "*A guy named Newman told me all about it.*" But just as he thought about sending that response, his connector shut down and would not come back on. "I must have broke it," he thought. But as soon as those words came to his mind, they showed up on the screen of his device and were instantly sent to Kakei. She responded with, "*Broke what?*" This was strange. He had never had a problem with his connector before. "What in the world?" Tru-man thought. And once again, his most recent thought showed up on the screen and was sent out by his connector.

He figured he'd better shut it off manually before it sent something he might be embarrassed about thinking. But first, he decided to communicate the message about Newman that didn't go through the first time. He thought it, and it showed up on the screen. But when he thought about sending it, once again, his connector shut down. By that time, Tru-man had made it home. He turned off his instant thought device and sat outside on the front steps of his building. Looking around at his neighbors, he wondered what those people were going to eat for dinner. He wondered how they could go on with their lives being satisfied with only the fast food they were used to. But then, it dawned on him that he too would have to go the rest of his life eating nothing but the fast food served in the city. He remembered what Newman told him as they sat around the table, "We won't be able to eat together like this again until the day I come back to the city. But every time you get together and eat with people who've been to this table, remember me. And look forward to the day when I'm back in the city. It's gonna be a feast like you've never seen!"

Tru-man got up and went inside where he was met by his brother, with whom he lived, and his sister who was visiting. "Where have you been Trumaine? We've been sending you messages since yesterday. Your job said you didn't come in today but that you've been leaving weird messages. Then one of your co-workers said you went up the hill?" He responded, "Didn't you get my instant thought a little while ago? I couldn't send any messages while I was on the hill but as soon as I got back, I sent out like a million thoughts." "Yeah, well none of them came to us," his brother shot back. "Is everybody else more important than your family?" his sister asked. "Nah," Tru-man replied, "look, I'll show you." He pulled out his connector and turned it on. He went to his sent thought messages which only had three messages in it; all three of them to his ex-girlfriend.

"Oh," his sister said, rolling her eyes, "You sent a million messages to Kakei, hunh? Well, let her worry about you from now on." Tru-man tried to win back his siblings affections, convincing them with, "Look, y'all know I love y'all. My connector is just broke. I sent so many messages today that it must have just bugged out. Kakei was one of the last people I messaged, that's why her messages are still there." Just then, his connector buzzed. A message came through. It was, of course, from Kakei. His siblings sighed in frustration. They didn't care much for Kakei or like the fact that Tru-man kept in touch with her after the two of them broke up. The message read, *"Okay Tru', I can't wait to hear all about this Newman and his soul food and anything else going on with you. Message me later."* Tru-man was not as hungry as he might have otherwise been, but he turned to his family and pleaded, "C'mon, let's go to Halfway's and get something to eat. I have something to tell you. No! Better yet, I have something I wanna show you."

They left the house to go eat; they had to since, they could not make a meal at home. None of the houses in Nameless City had a kitchen or any place to store or prepare food. Halfway's-house was a fast food chain—the only fast food chain—in the city, responsible for feeding all the citizens. Every day, people looked forward to eating there but not because the food was so great. In fact, the food always looked twice as good on the menu as it actually was when it was finally served. Some joked that this was what the name "Halfway's" stood for— meals that were only half-way cooked or half as good as advertised. Another running joke was that the best place to live in Nameless City was right next to Halfway's because the food never completely satisfied anyone and therefore, no one could go more than a couple of hours before needing to rush back to the restaurant in order to eat again.

And yet, the people of Nameless City always looked forward to eating there because the restaurant had the greatest commercials. And every commercial advertised a new recipe, guaranteeing that customers would finally know what it feels like to be satisfied. But that never seemed to happen. There were even rumors that the food caused a kind of temporary insanity because, not long after eating it, people were tempted to do great harm to themselves or to others. On top of that disturbing trend, it always seemed as if life in Nameless City was only half as good as it could be; people were only half as kind as they felt they should be; relationships lasted only half as long as they otherwise would and the streets were only half as safe as the citizens might have liked them to be. But all of this was dismissed as merely a strange coincidence.

As Tru-man traveled with his siblings, the tension was still somewhat in the air. His brother and sister, walking on either side of him, wanted him to feel the emotional sting for having neglected them. Meanwhile Tru-man, feeling the heat in the middle, could hardly contain himself as he waited for an opportunity to share about his hilltop experiences. After walking silently, dodging one another's eyes for several city blocks, his brother finally broke the sound barrier, "Well, are you gonna tell us what happen on the hill or do we have to wait 'til you get your connecter fixed?" The siblings began to laugh as they pushed and bumped Tru-man back and forth between them like a living Newton's Cradle.

Tru-man laughed. Then his mouth began functioning like his broken connector. Every thought that popped into his head concerning the hill, the restaurant, the food, the service, the living artwork on the walls of the restaurant and more, spilled out of his mouth in an almost breathless blog of details. In his excitement, Tru-man almost missed his brother and sister leaning forward to make eye contact with one another, raising their eyebrows to imply that maybe their big brother had come back down the hill with more than just a burned out connector. Perhaps he himself had sustained a mental meltdown.

Tru-man stopped and said, "Look y'all, I know this sounds a little crazy, but unless you've been up there, you're just not going to understand. But man! I wish you would just . . . I want y'all to think about taking the trip up." He knew it would take more than that though. Ever since they were young, they had heard all kinds of myths and mysteries about the many hills surrounding the city. There was not much truth to any of them. But the stories were so old and so odd that it was commonly thought that only the most daring or desperate individuals would even try to make a trip up any of the nearby hills.

They finally arrived at Halfway's-house and after waiting for a while, finally got in. As they sat down and looked over the menu, Tru-man couldn't get excited about anything on it. Had he not been so distracted, he might have realized how similar the menu was to the one given him at the restaurant he visited halfway up the hill. But he just kept thinking about the top of the hill. Then he remembered that he had a menu in his back pocket from Newman and his father's restaurant. "Wait," he said. "Check this out. Here's what I wanted to show you." He pulled out the menu and set it down on the table then, watched as he waited for them to experience what he had when he first read the menu. He smiled expectantly, looking back and forth from one sibling to the other but, much to his disappointment, nothing happened.

"It's very nice," his sister said. "Did you design this or something? How long did it take you?" his brother inquired. "How could I have designed this?" Tru-man asked. It was a very elaborate menu. "Nothing?" Tru-man probed. His brother and sister once again looked at one another, as if, to question their big brother's mental health. "Cut it out," Tru-man warned as he snatched back the menu. Unbeknownst to him, his brother and sister could not experience what he had because the air was too dense with the odor of fast food. On the hill, the air is much more pure. But in the city, it helps to find places where the atmosphere is not so polluted if the aroma therapy of the menu or a gust of wind from the hill is going to have much of an effect.

They ordered and ate their meal as happily as they could, but Tru-man could not finish his meal. For one thing, he was not hungry; but also, he noticed that he no longer enjoyed the taste of what was served in that place. As they returned home, Tru-man found himself in the middle of his brother and sister again but, this time, there were no smiles. He got between them in order to break up a vicious argument that almost turned into a physical fight. This was strange because Tru-man was playing the role of peace maker. Usually, after leaving Halfway's, all three of the siblings would be forced to go separate ways because of their hostility toward one another.

It was now late. Tru-man, concerned for his sister's safety, convinced her to spend the night by giving up his room and going to sleep on the couch. Perhaps it was because she was not in her own bed or, maybe it was the fact that she was still hungry, whatever the reason she could not sleep. In the middle of the night, she went into the living room to see if Tru-man was still awake only to find him sound asleep. But, there on the floor beside him, she spotted his menu and decided to look it over. She stood, quietly reading it aloud while trying not to wake him. Looking down at her brother on the couch, she smiled before returning the menu to the floor, and then returning to bed.

The next morning, Tru-man got up and went in to work. Once he reached the entrance, he turned on his connector in order to register at the front office but was surprised to learn that he no longer had a job. At least, that's what the system reported after syncing with his connector. The administrator tried typing in several different codes in order to manually log him in but nothing worked. "I've been having trouble with my connector since yesterday. I gotta go get it fixed," Tru-man explained. But he was told, "I'm sorry sir, until your connector reads differently there's nothing I can do." "Can I at least speak to my boss?" Tru-man requested. "Sure sir, have a seat and I'll try to reach him."

He sat down and began sending out instant thought messages to his co-workers explaining that he would not be at his work station for a second straight day. His connector, all of a sudden, was working perfectly. One of his co-workers replied, *"I know. I came in this morning and there was already somebody else working in your spot. I heard that you sent a message saying you quit yesterday after you came back from up the hill so I just figured you had lost your mind or something. LOL"*

This worried Tru-man. It was one thing for his connector to be short circuiting and sending out thoughts of his that he never intended to send; it was quite another for it to be sending out thoughts that never even entered his mind. Mr. Taskman, his boss, came to the front of the office and looked at him very carefully. "Trumaine, are you feeling okay? We're not going to have a problem are we?" "Problem? What do you mean?" Tru-man shot back. "The only problem is you've hired someone else and no one has said a word to me about it. Is this because I left early two days ago and then didn't come in yesterday? I know I should've called in but I really couldn't. But I'm sure I had enough time stored up to be able to take off."

"No." Mr. Taskman informed him, "It's not just that you took off yesterday. It's what you said when you got back. You disrespected your supervisor and me. You quit and told us if we ever see you around the city we'd better turn and walk the other way. You young guys are so careless. You send out these rude instant thoughts on your connectors and then you expect not to have to pay the consequences. And now you think I should just give you your job back and pretend you never thought those things about me?"

Tru-man jumped in pleading, "Mr. Taskman, have you ever had any problems out of me? I didn't send those instant thoughts. I didn't quit. My connector just started bugging out on me yesterday when I came back from up the hill. I sent a bunch of messages, more than I ever sent out at one time before and then, when I went to send out the last one, it shut down." Mr. Taskman came back with, "Oh yeah, what was the last message? Is that the one where you threatened to burn this company down?" "No!" Tru-man shouted in frustration. "It was about Newman!"

Instantly, Tru-man remembered what Newman told him, "When you get back to the city, you might have some trouble because of me. I'm not remembered kindly down there, if at all." Breaking his concentration, Mr. Taskman scoffed, "Newman? I should've known something crazy was happening. How else could you have gotten one of your chains removed? Everybody who comes back from meeting him goes insane. Did you ask him why he and his father won't take these chains off of us down here?

Or why he only took off one of your chains? Or why he won't let anybody come back down the hill in his or her right mind? My mother and my brother went up there and ain't been right since. Get outta here and take that garbage to Gehenna!" Gehenna was the city's trash heap. It burned continually at the opposite end of the city from where the great hill sat. All of the city's left over fast food was taken there at the end of every week. Because it served this destructive purpose, people began using the name Gehenna as a colorful form of condemnation.

Tru-man left the office and went to clean out his locker. He passed his co-workers but did not know what to say. As they looked at him, some wondered if he had indeed lost his mind. Others looked as if they were mere seconds away from violently jumping on him. "Say it to my face," one of them shouted. "My connector is broke. I didn't say . . . I didn't think any of that stuff!" he screamed. But he was shown no mercy. Once in the locker room, he stood motionless, thinking of how he could undo the damage of the last twenty-four hours. But if he could undo it, would he also have to undo his time spent at Newman's table? Would he wish that undone?

As he pondered these things, his co-worker Jermaine entered. "Hey man," Jermaine said sympathetically. "Looks like you put on some weight at the top of that hill, hunh?" "Yeah," Tru-man replied, "but I ain't know my trip was gonna be weighing on me like this." Then Jermaine began to inquire, "Forgive me for asking man but. . ." He paused, not knowing how to ask what he really wanted to know. "What?" Tru-man demanded. Jermaine found the only words he could, "Uhm . . . Are you crazy now?" Tru-man laughed. Jermaine laughed, even as he watched Tru-man carefully just to be safe. "Do you think I'm crazy?" Tru-man answered by asking.

"Well," Jermained quizzed, "Do you see invisible lions chasing you? Are you in love with some mysterious chic up on the hill? Are you gonna spend the rest of your life talking about how good the soul food restaurant at the top of the hill is?" Jermaine laughed, waiting for Tru-man to reassure him that his laughter was appropriate. Tru-man laughed a little and then got somewhat serious as he responded, "No and no." Realizing that Tru-man only offered two "no"s after being asked three questions, Jermaine leaned in and asked, "The food was that good hunh?" Tru-man's face lit up.

He spent the next forty-five minutes telling Jermaine about every aspect of his journey and experience on the hill. He showed him the menu and watched, hoping to witness that strange filling phenomenon take place with Jermaine as it had with him on the hill. And it did. After experiencing the miracle of the menu, Jermaine had even more questions. Tru-man could've talked more and Jermaine would've listened, but Tru-man got an instant thought from Kakei asking, *"What are you doing? You never answered my question yesterday about Newman."* Tru-man read the message but was shocked as he noticed the time. He apologized to Jermaine, "I'm sorry man. I've kept you from your job. And I gotta go get my connector fixed. That's why all this mess is happening. My ex-girl seems to be one of the only people I can communicate with without issues."

The two friends shook hands and then Tru-man left through the exit leading back to the side street of the building. Jermaine had been so caught up in Tru-man's story that he forgot to tell him what he went into the locker room to say. He pulled out his connector and tried to locate Tru-man's dot but could not. So he thought the words, *"Tru' if you're reading this message, that mean's your connector is fixed. Holla at me. There's something I need to tell you about your trip up the hill—Jermaine."* He sent the message and then went back to work.

Tru-man thought about responding to Kakei, but he figured he'd better get his connector fixed first. He thought too, for a moment, that perhaps there was some sort of conspiracy; that mentioning the name of Newman was enough to make the media center shut his connector down. But he countered that thought with, "Maybe I'm just being paranoid. After all, Kakei just mentioned Newman and nothing happened." He made his way to the media center and stood in the long line at service window five, the shortest line there was.

Tru-man was so used to living life through his connector that he forgot that his wasn't working properly. He pulled it out and was about to send a message but, upon looking at the screen, he remembered why he was in the line in the first place. So instead of sending any instant thoughts, he switched his connector to public and signed into the public dot room to see what other people around him were talking about. This was a common practice. Most people in Nameless City set their instant thought status on "public" so they would always be able to meet new people. As he read the many messages being sent and posted, it saddened him that no one was thinking or talking about anything that had to do with what happens on the hilltop.

Just then, he noticed a security guard walking swiftly across the room to go break up a small crowd that had gathered. As the guard returned and the crowd dispersed, the woman behind Tru-man asked one of the participants, "What was that all about?" The man responded, "Some girl over there was talking about that soul food joint up at the top of the hill on the north end of the city. She was pretty convincing too. Almost made me want to go." Tru-man looked but could not see who it was that had drawn the small crowd. So he left his line and went to go stand by the window on the other side of the room, near where the crowd had gathered. He thought that, perhaps, the girl had come to the media center because of the same connector problems he was having after returning from the hill. And he was right.

He listened carefully to each conversation at the customer service window for the next fifteen minutes and then, finally, heard a young woman say, "Yes, I'm here because my connector is crazy, okay?" She laughed and continued, "I used to work for the company that makes these. I know how to build'em and how to fix'em, but y'all got some new kinda software on this bad boy and I just don't have the time. Okay?" And she laughed. "What seems to be the problem ma'am?" a lady from behind the glass asked. The joyful young woman responded, "Well it seems like it's got a mind of its own—saying stuff I didn't say. And then, when I wanna say something, especially about what I went through on the hill, all of a sudden it shuts down. Let me found out y'all got a problem with my man Newman, okay? " She laughed again.

Tru-man was drawn to her playful forwardness. The response from behind the glass came, "Okay miss, we're sorry for the inconvenience. If you want to leave your connector with us you can pick it back up in about an hour. Your name please?" Tru-man listened harder now. The young woman replied, "Angelique." How fitting was her name, Tru-man thought to himself, for she was quite angelic. After she left the window, Tru-man jumped into the front of the line and tossed his connector to the media service rep, saying quickly, "I have the same problem. Put it with hers. Be back in an hour. Trumaine." Then he ran and caught up with Angelique.

"So, you've dined with Newman?" he asked. She looked him directly in the eyes, attempting to discern whether he was being sincere or sarcastic. "What do you know about it?" she quipped. "Well, he let me keep this," Tru-man replied as he pulled out his menu. Angelique smiled and asked, "So have you been to any of Newman's chain restaurants here in the city?" "What?" Tru-man, stunned by the thought, stopped in his tracks and then caught back up with her to respond, "Newman said we couldn't eat like that again until he returned to the city. I was just there yesterday. There's no way he's back here already and got chain restaurants set up!" "No," she countered, "of course not. On the bottom of every page in the menu there's a scent guide that helps you know when you're getting close to a place that serves Newman's style of cuisine. Most times it's in someone's home."

With a puzzled look on his face, Tru-man probed deeper. "Why not just have an address listed for the spots? If Newman isn't there, what's the point? And how are people making meals in their homes? Only the Halfway's-houses have kitchens." She began to explain, "Well you're right, Newman isn't there. But just like the aroma comes and something fills you up when you read the menu, the same thing happens when people who've been to Newman's table get together and reflect on what's in the menu. And no, it's not as good as what we had when we were with him, but it's a million times better than the Halfway's fast food. That stuff is made for Gehenna! Okay?"

She laughed and continued, "And I don't know how they're making these meals in their homes. It just seems like whenever two or three of us get together, all the ingredients and things we need for cooking just happen to be present too. One person has this ingredient; another person has such and such a thing that we just happen to need. Sometimes people don't even know they have the missing ingredient until it's needed. But everyone has something and the meals taste better when each person contributes their piece. It's wild. So maybe the reason there's no address listed is because it could happen anywhere Newman's friends are gathered."

Tru-man thought about these things. He really wanted to know how the scent guide worked and how close these places in the city came to the original restaurant. He asked, "Are you hungry now? How bout we find one of those spots to have lunch?" Jokingly, she replied, "Are you asking me on a date?" And quite seriously, he replied, "Yeah. I think I am." And so, they opened the menu and followed the guide until they came to a store front café serving a small lunch crowd. They went in and took their places at the table but Tru-man got up and pulled an extra chair over to the table beside him. They did not have to order anything. After talking for a while with the other guests, food was brought out and set before them and they received it with gladness. The meal did remind them of Newman's table, but it left a lot to be desired. Angelique, looking slightly embarrassed, remarked that, "Some places remind you of Newman's table more than others. But none of them gets it quite perfect."

Tru-man noticed that there were no prices listed. "How much do we owe?" he asked. But Angelique informed him. "It's free. Remember how on the hill, Newman paid everybody's bill? Well the same applies here." This confused Tru-man. "Then why is everybody pulling out money?" he asked. But she explained that people were not paying, rather, they were supporting the restaurant; giving what they could so that it could remain open, improve the quality of service and do a better job of imitating and representing the original hilltop restaurant.

As they walked back to the media center, they exchanged stories about how they came to journey up the hill. Tru-man told of his adventure first. Then Angelique began, "I just came back from up the hill about a month ago. My parents tried to take me there once when I was younger, but my dad had his soul fooled about halfway up. Me and my mom never made it to the top. We came back down to the city to live on fast food. She's been running from the lions ever since. She says that I saw them too, but I don't remember. I guess I was too young. Then one day, about three months ago, a friend of mine went up there. And when he got back, he couldn't stop talking about the food. So after hearing him enough I just said, 'you know what? I tried to go up and didn't make it when I was younger, but that was really my parents' decision, not mine.' I just had a feeling that it would be different if I went up because I wanted to go and not because they made me, you know?" Tru-man nodded in agreement.

She continued, "So I went up. And I made it!" But Tru-man challenged her rendition, "Did you 'make it' or did Newman rescue you and practically carry you to the top?" Angelique laughed; she was always laughing. She confessed, "I see you really have been with Newman. Okay, you got me. He rescued me and took me to the top of the hill. And I loved it. I love Newman. Anyway, when I got back I began having problems. I mean, at first it was great. I was satisfied all day long. Plus, I was saving tons of money because I stopped eating at Halfway's-house. I mean, you might catch me there every once in a while; but no body's perfect right?"

She laughed and then continued, "But people started thinking that I was conceited because I didn't want to just eat fast food. And I was always getting together with other people who had been to Newman's table. My friends started blaming me for the loss of some of our other friends who went up the hill after me but haven't come back yet. And even though I never liked using my connector, it's like you

HAVE to use'em these days. But now, all of a sudden, my connector starts bugging out and causing me problems at work, with family and all kinds of drama."

Tru-man began rubbing his chin like he was putting together pieces of a puzzle in his head. He thought out loud, "You know, I wonder if the reason there are no addresses in the menu is because of what Newman said. Didn't he say that we might have trouble in the city because of him? And you and I both have had trouble with our connectors after talking about the hill or Newman. Maybe something really is going on. We need to get our connectors back and see what's really happening." They hurried back to the media center and went to the pickup window. After retrieving their connectors they rushed outside to begin a series of tests. First, they sent instant thoughts to one another, to friends and their families. They waited for and received responses. The messages contained nothing about the hill or Newman or soul food. There connectors seemed to be back to normal.

Next they sent messages to people containing the words "hill," "new," and "man" but in no specific context relating to their experiences with Newman. Tru-man suggested that she send an instant thought to one of her friends announcing, "*Angelique has a new man."* She thought he was very cleverly flirting with her. And she was right. Nonetheless, she sent the message. Once again, the message went through with no problems and she received a response which simply asked, *"What are you talking about girl?"* Angelique responded with the instant thought, *"I meant to say, you've got to read this new menu from my man Newman's restaurant."* She thought it, and the words appeared on the screen of her connector. But as she thought about sending it, her device went blank and shut off.

Tru-man was getting ready to send a message about Newman to Kakei but, before he could think it, he received an instant thought which said, *"Tru' if you're reading this message, that mean's your connector is fixed. Holla at me. There's something I need to tell you about your trip up the hill— Jermaine."* Tru-man responded, *"My Maine-man,"* (That's what he called Jermaine) *"I got your message. Whassup?"* Jermaine received Tru-man's message and thought to reply with:

After we talked a couple of days ago, I went and asked my Grandmom about you taking a trip up the hill. She told me that not everyone comes back down the hill in their right mind, just like I told you. But then she said that those who come back with their right hand unchained will never fit in down here again because of some guy named Newman. She said the people who run the media and the jobs, especially the job we do, have a huge vendetta against Newman for some reason. Like, they get something out of keeping him out of the city. And I was here yesterday when Mr. Taskman got your instant thought about quitting. He was angry. But he said he couldn't fire you because of your work contract with the city and that you couldn't quit your job through a connector device. He said you had to actually come in and sign a form to terminate your contract. But when we came in this morning, to my surprise and to his delight, the city had terminated your contract for some other reason and had already hired a replacement for you without Taskman even knowing. It looks like someone with a little bit of power doesn't like you very much so be careful. I could really use something to eat, so I'm gonna go. I'll catch you later—Jermaine.

All of these words appeared on the screen of his connector, but just as he thought about sending this message to Tru-man, Jermaine's connector went blank and shut down. Tru-man waited several minutes for a response from him but none came. As he waited he received an instant thought from Kakei. He read it aloud, "*Trumaine, why haven't you answered me? I really want to hear about your trip up the hill, about the underground mall and this Newman guy.*" Angelique commented, "Trumaine? I never even asked your name but now I know." "Tru-man," he offered. "My friends call me Tru-man." She smiled at the new information but something bothered her.

"Why didn't her phone shut off when she mentioned Newman?" Angelique asked. Tru-man thought for a moment and replied, "You know, it's weird. Ever since I came back down the hill, she's the only person I've been able to send instant thoughts to without my phone shutting down. I mean, well it shut down the first time I mentioned Newman to her. But after that, it's been straight." "She a good friend of yours?" Angelique inquired. "Well," Tru-man said nervously, "She's my ex. But she's really curious to learn about what happened on the hill." Sensing the need to show that he could distance himself from Kakei, he added, "I'm gonna answer her later." "No," Angelique replied. "I wouldn't want to see anybody miss out on what we found up there." And so, Tru-man sent Kakei an instant thought that read, "*Sorry for taking so long to get back to you. What are you doing right now*?" "*Not much. I want to see you and catch up*," Kakei sent back.

Tru-man turned to Angelique and proposed the idea, "You said that whenever two or three people who've been to Newman's table get together, they just happen to have all the ingredients and necessities for preparing a meal, right? Why don't we get some people together tonight? I can invite Kakei and my man Maine. He seemed very interested in going up the hill when we talked earlier." Angelique agreed that this would be a good idea, so Tru-man searched for Jermaine's location in his connector and saw that he was still at work. He was about to send a message telling Jermaine that he was coming by the job with some friends but he decided that it would be better to just surprise him with the soul food social right as he was getting off from work.

He and Angelique walked to Kakei's house to collect her. Next, they walked to some of Angelique's friends' homes to invite them as well. As they walked, the group talked about their time up the hill and some of the problems they encountered after returning. Meanwhile, Kakei trailed behind them, occupied by her connector, sending and receiving instant thoughts. They arrived at Tru-man's old job where he snuck them in through the side door that led to the locker room, and then to the employee break room. He looked out at Jermaine's work station but did not see him so he pulled out his connector to locate him. "According to this," Tru-man said, sounding slightly confused, "He's in the locker room. But we just came through there." Tru-man went back into the locker room and moved slowly until he came to stand directly over the spot where his connector told him he could find Jermaine. It was a trashcan.

Buzzing and lighting up inside the can was Jermaine's connector. Tru-man pulled it out and saw an "unsent message" alert on the screen. He wondered if the unsent message was meant for him. He selected, "open" and read the message about Newman that Jermaine tried to send to him before his phone shut down. His heart began racing. Tru-man walked slowly back into the break room and sat down. "What's wrong Tru'?" Angelique and Kakei asked at the same time. It was an awkward moment for the two young ladies. "I think something may have happen to Maine," he said. Then he told them about the message Jermaine tried to send him and how he found his connector in the trash.

"I don't think we're safe here." Tru-man said, almost whispering. "I think it would be a good idea if we all turned off our connectors for a while." But Angelique's friends had already learned to live without them and therefore, did not even have connectors with them. Tru-man turned his off and then looked at Kakei. "Hold on," she said. "Just let me tell my parents where I am. I know I'm grown, but they still worry." Angelique chimed in, "Yeah, that's a good idea. Let me do that too just in case." But

Angelique's connector had been off for over an hour, ever since it shut down when she tried to send the message to her friend about Newman. She was really attempting to turn her connector on, hoping that Kakei's instant thought status was set to public and not private. And it was. Angelique's connector came on just in enough time for her to locate Kakei and read her public message. Angelique read aloud what Kakei thought she was sending secretly, *"I'm here at the tree-felling factory with Tru-man and four other 'free-hands.' If you want to catch them off guard and catch them in the act, come within the hour—Kakei."*

Everyone's eyes locked on Kakei, who got up and shot towards the door. But Angelique blocked the way while Tru-man came from behind her and snatched away her connector. He read the message again, not wanting to believe that she could really be spying on their gathering. He demanded to know, "What's going on Kakei? Who are you sending this to?" "No one," she said defensively. "Just some friends who heard you went up the hill. They were curious. I was inviting them to join us. Just give me back my connector and I'll tell them not to come. It'll be alright." Tru-man held the connector back behind his body. He turned around and began checking the connector to see who the recipients of the message were.

"Forty recipients!?!" he shouted. "Why are you telling forty people that we're here and that they could catch us 'in the act'?" "Alright," she shouted back at him. "I'll tell you what happened but please Trumaine, don't be mad at me. Listen. Remember when you sent me the message yesterday about being on the hill and I asked you about the rumors, about the underground mall? Well, I really did wanna know. But then I never heard back from you. Then, later, I got a message from the city saying something about a free shopping spree. A trip to that underground mall people used to talk about and that I'd be able to come back with as much free stuff as I could bag, drag or carry.

"I thought it was a joke but then they mentioned you. Said all I had to do was keep tabs on you; find out when and where you were going to eat and with whom. I didn't wanna do it cuz, you know, I love you. But then they said you were about to commit some kind of treason against the city and that anybody with one free hand was part of this big conspiracy. They said some guy named Newman had freed y'all up just enough to be able to help him, but not enough so that you could fight back against him. They told me they were gonna help protect y'all from Newman so y'all wouldn't have to help him anymore. I didn't know what to believe but they said if I didn't help them, I'd be charged with treason too."

Just then, her connector buzzed with an alert. "It's them. It's the city." Kakei said. Tru-man clicked the connector and read the message, *"Is Newman inside? Is he coming? We can't come in if Newman is there."* He turned to Kakei, "Is that what they think, that Newman is coming? Good, they won't come in if they think he's here," he said as he paced back and forth thinking. "We're leaving," he said. "Where are we going?" Kakei asked. But Angelique answered, "You're not going anywhere." Tru-man confirmed, "She's right Kakei. If you come, they'll think we took you hostage or that you've become one of us. Either way, it's a bad idea. But we're taking your connector. They've done something to it that allows you to send messages about Newman and not get shut down. If it's not in the signature card then we should be able to switch connectors but keep our own ID cards, that way, I'll be able to communicate as myself from your connector. Listen Kakei. Newman *is* coming. If you help us, I'll make sure he knows that you did." Tru-man did not know when, or think it would be soon, but he did believe that Newman would return to the city.

Kakei stood silently, considering her options. "Listen," Tru-man said. "There is an underground mall but the city can't get to it. And even when they do get help to bring things out from the mall, the stuff never makes it past Gehenna. I can't explain it all now. But you've gotta trust me. Newman is the only one who can bring things out from the mall without destroying them in the process. Will you help us?" The look of hurt and desperation in the eyes of the others in the room began to weigh on her. She shook her head, "Okay. What do you want me to do?"

At that moment, a rock flew through the window and a crowd could be heard yelling for "traitors" to come out before the mob decided to come in. Tru-man began switching the ID cards in the connectors. Moving frantically, he laid out the plan. "Alright, wait two minutes and then send a message to your contacts in the city saying that Newman was here but you're not sure where he went. Say that you're going to go look for him. Then, after five more minutes, send another instant thought saying that we tricked you. Say that everyone left through the rooftops and headed north toward the great hill."

He handed her his connector which now contained her ID card. "I'll contact you soon using some kind of code. Kakei, please be strong." He gave her his menu and left the room with Angelique and her friends. But they did not go up the stairs to the roof to head north. Tru-man thought the city might have the road to the hill blocked off. Instead, he took his friends down to the basement and entered the tunnels heading south to the other end of the city— to Gehenna. They ran for quite a while. The stench of trash and corroding fast food being sent southbound with them was almost unbearable. Tru-man slowed down enough to ask those running with him to give him the names of everyone they knew who had been to the top of hill. He entered the names and created a group-list in his new connector. Then he sent out the following instant thought:

Dinner with Friends

To all those who've had the high honor of sitting at the highest table; to all those who no longer enjoy dining down in the city; to all those who have had a hard time connecting through your connectors: tonight you will learn that we are called conspirators, but the truth is that there is a conspiracy against us. The free hand that you used to eat at Newman's table is now seen as a raised fist against this city. I do not know what will happen if they catch us dining together, enjoying our New friend's very present absence, but I don't think we want to find out either. In the Halfway's-house they say, "If you can't stand the heat get out of the kitchen." Friends of Newman, we must STAND the HEAT. Jump with us, out of the city's frying pan and into the FIRE. If you make it, your New friends WOOD be NEAR waiting to receive you with free handed fellowship.

P.S. Do not RSVP!

This was an invitation to all of Newman's friends to meet in the woods down by Gehenna. He sent the message and watched it go through to all 117 recipients. "I hope this works. I hope they get it," he said, second guessing his coded communication. He turned off his new connector and then, picking back up his pace, continued traveling down the underground tunnel toward its bright and terrible destination.

By the Fires of Gehenna

After walking and talking with Newman for about an hour, I noticed that a wondrous thing had been happening to me. After he helped me turn away from the SOUL FOOLED restaurant, it took a while for my heart to completely turn away from the beautiful waitress there who tried to place me on a platter and serve me to Curse and Consequence.

"How's that sound?" Tru-man asked. "It's intriguing. And it's worded well," Pitman responded. "But are you sure you wanna start your book off in the middle of the story like that?" Tru-man met Pitman after about three months of living as a fugitive in the woods on the outskirts of Gehenna. Pitman and Tru-man had become close friends in the month since he and his wife arrived. He had not yet made the trip up the great hill to Newman's table, and so both of his hands were still chained. His wife, however, had been and he promised her that he too would go someday. But for now, he followed her into the woods to be a part of the new community being led by Tru-man.

At first, only about twenty-five people responded to Tru-man's instant thought message to meet by the "FIRE." Many didn't trust the authenticity of the message. Others did not receive it because they had stopped using their connectors. And still, there were others who wanted to come, but were caught by city agents and jailed for treason. During the day, the "Free-hand-fellowship" (as they came to call themselves) spent most of their time roaming the woods, looking for food and cooking materials or building shelters and hiding them well.

Tru-man put together a team of scouts, whose job it was to go back into the city during the day in order to eavesdrop on conversations and bring back news of the city's plans concerning "Free-hands." Their duties also included finding Free-hands who were still living in the city undercover; discovering the fate of those who had been jailed, in order that they might try to help them; and also, they were responsible for carving signs in trees that said, "F-H-F" with a flame beside or underneath it. This was an invitation for Free-hands or future Free-hands to join them near Gehenna.

One young man, named Cartman, was charged with the duty of carrying Tru-man's messages to Kakei. His job was to go into the city, turn on Tru-man's connector and post one or two words as an instant thought in a publicly viewed message room. He would then tag over fifty random people to alert them of his post. When Kakei saw the activity alert on Tru-man's dot display page, she would click in to read the message. Then she would wait, while Cartman turned off the connector (so he couldn't be tracked) and moved to a different location to post another message with one or two more words. He would continue this until Tru-man's entire message to her was delivered.

At first, once a message was fully posted, it would take Kakei about half an hour to decode it. But she soon got much faster. Kakei would respond with a public post just as quickly as she could think of a code for what she wanted to say. But she had to begin posting random thoughts on her dot display page six to eight times a day so that it would not look like she was always only posting thoughts after Tru-man's messages showed up online. All of this was Tru'man's plan to keep her from being suspected of helping or having any kind of contact with the Free-hand-fellowship.

Interpreting Kakei's posts was difficult at first. Over time, Tru-man learned that "pain in my hand" meant there would be a raid on suspected Free-hand hideouts in the woods. "Right hand" meant the city was coming from the east and "left hand" meant the west. "Last week" or "last Thursday" meant "next week" or "next Thursday." And for Thursday of the current week, her warnings would begin with "A year ago this Thursday." Several Free-hands were arrested near Gehenna and Tru-man himself was almost captured once when one of Kakei's posts was misinterpreted by the F-H-F. This was no way to live, but what choice did they have?

Angelique poked her head into Tru-man's hideout and asked, "How's the book coming?" "It's coming I guess," he sighed. "The ideas are there, but I can't seem to get the beginning right." But she assured him, "I'm sure it'll come to you. The scouts are back though; you may wanna come here this." Tru-man climbed out of his den, followed by Pitman. The scouts marched into the makeshift campsite and began broadcasting their news. Cartman announced, "I think they might be on to us with the trees. Some of the ones that we marked have been completely cut down. And others have had our mark crossed out and the letters N.I.N.T.E. carved there instead, spelled on an angle slanting up. Maybe that's how they're marking the trees to be cut down. And we found seven more Free-hands. Three have been very clever, strategizing ways to persuade others to take the risk of going up the hill. Two others have never revealed their free hand to anyone. They say they're afraid to be found out and want to try to keep their lives the way they were before all of this drama jumped off."

"And the other two?" Tru-man inquired. "They came back with us," Cartman said. "They're over there, torching their connectors in the great fire." Tru-man stood, shaking his head up and down slowly. "Alright," he said. "There's one more thing," Cartman prefaced. "The city put out a warning that all Free-handed people have twenty-four hours to register with the city. I don't know what happens if they find someone who hasn't registered after tomorrow." Tru-man rubbed his head, thinking of ways to encourage his new community. But he had no words. He dismissed the gathering and then turned to his inner circle and delegated, "It's getting dark. Pitman, help our new friends understand the rules." "No doubt," Pitman replied.

As he walked away, Cartmen pulled Tru-man to the side and said quietly, "Hey man, I didn't want to say anything to the gathering cuz I'm not sure what it means. But Kakei said she got word from a good source that something is happening starting tomorrow morning. She doesn't know what but it has to do with your old job, and it affects us." "Okay," Tru-man said, looking past Cartman as if the answer was somewhere in the trees behind him. "Good call, thanks."

As the night set in, the free handed society gathered together for a meal. It had become their custom as they sat around to leave an empty place at their makeshift tables for Newman. This was done to commemorate him and to help each of them stay mindful of their hope of dining with him again when he returned to the city. After dinner, Angelique and Tru-man took a walk along a path of trees that had become very familiar to the two of them. Even though it was dark, they knew their way back to the campsite. Though they were more friends than anything, it was clear to everyone in the camp that they had fallen in love. On this particular night, as they reached their turn around mark and began to make their way back, Tru-man paused and then spoke. "I don't know how to say this," he began. Angelique smiled with anticipation that was hidden in the night. "I have desires," Tru-man continued. "And when I try to put those desires into words, I can only think of one word; one very soft, powerful word." She dared not break his concentration or interrupt his speech with even a breath. He uttered the only word he could, "You."

Once his secret was out, the two love-struck friends switched roles. It was her turn to speak and he was now the breathless one. His heart agreed with his bated breath; even its beating would wait until after her response. She leaned forward and touched her forehead to his. Her lips parted as she little more than whispered, "It seems no matter what you're doing, no matter how far or how close you are, I always want to be closer." Tru-man breathed again. Relieved that the feelings he had were mutual. He planned out loud, "No matter how far in the future I see myself, I always see you when I see me." "So what does that mean? What do we do now?" she asked. He thought for a second and then suggested, "When we get back to the camp, we should find an older couple; a married couple and ask them what they think about our love in light of our current situation. I don't want us to go causing ourselves a lot of pain in the future, just because we want the pleasure of each other now." She agreed that this would be wise as the fingers of their free hands found one another and interlocked. Holding hands, they happily made their way back to the camp.

Tru-man watched Angelique go into her hideout and then, he scouted out a spot for himself to sit. He found the perfect place; close enough that the great fire which burned continually could give him sufficient light for his writing project, but not so close that he was forced to inhale the full essence of that place. He picked up his pen and pad and then picked up where he had left off.

> *But it eventually dawned on me that I was no longer thinking about returning to love that beautiful woman who hated my soul. I had been listening to Newman talk and forgotten all about her. And then I realized that, somehow, I was able to forget that I was even walking. With each step I took, I had gotten lighter and lighter on my feet. The higher up the hill we went, it was as though the air was filling with helium, or filling me with helium. But it didn't make me talk strange. Instead, it inflated my internal organs and lifted me like a balloon. Even though I was moving my feet, it was like I*

was floating with Newman to the top of the hill. And as we got even higher, it was as if the helium was mixed with nitrous oxide—indeed—laughing gas. And just like nitrous oxide smells and tastes sweet, and brings laughter when inhaled; each breath I took was like consuming an airborne appetizer that served to make me increasingly aware of how much joy was waiting for me at the top of the hill.

All the while, Newman was talking, but he wasn't talking to me. It was more like he was talking through me. I could actually see his speech causing the air to vibrate, so that, I did not just hear him, rather I felt every word he spoke resonating at my core. So much that I could not, even in the slightest, deny the truth of what he said. And when he spoke about the past, the air did more than vibrate. It made shapes to illustrate the things he said. I could literally see what he was saying when he told me:

"A long time ago, way before you were born, one of my first customers named (H)Uman (the "H" is silent) got married in my restaurant. I catered the whole wedding and even the honeymoon. Wherever they

went, even down in the city where you live now, I had my soul's food tables set up to satisfy them. As a wedding present, I gave them the entire city. I sent them down there to live and to build it up any way they wanted. I had a mall built beneath the city and filled it with all types of valuable things: precious metals, stones and minerals. Uman and his wife had the privilege of shopping at any store in that mall. They could buy materials and everything they needed to build and furnish their homes. But I had a specific blueprint for one room in every house—the room where meals were to be prepared.

"I wanted to ensure that they would only eat healthy, soul nourishing meals; meals that would satisfy them at the deepest level of their longing and desire. I never intended for them to live on the fast food served in the city's Halfway's-houses. If they would have designed their kitchens according to my health code I would have come to each home, even to their children and their children's children, to teach them how to prepare my meals. And I would dine with them and they could dine with me as often as they wished.

"I wanted them to get used to coming toward me before they went toward material things, so I made the entrance to the mall halfway up the hill. You would have seen it on the road if that cursed café were not blocking the way. My employees worked in the mall. In every store, they stood to gladly serve Uman and his wife Evelyn. There was even a delivery system set up where Uman could enter the mall through the hillside, and then have my employees bring the goods to his home through the back of the mall which is all the way at the far end of your city, where Gehenna now is.

"But one day, one of my employees, an ambitious low-level clerk, somehow convinced himself that I never had plans to come to the city; that I was content to remain distant, up at the top of the hill. He thought that if he could get Uman and Evelyn to build their homes in a way that left me out, that he could then make them dependent on him for their food and nourishment. He wanted to rule the city from the mall's entrance, halfway up the hill; the same way he thought I planned to only rule it from the hilltop.

"About one-third of my employees bought into his plan. But the rest left the mall and came back to the top of the hill. My father fired the low-level clerk. This should have been a wakeup call to him but the clerk continued to put his plan in action. The first step was for him to trap Uman and Evelyn between the mall and the city so that my restaurant and the higher end of the hill were no longer an option. My father foresaw this and knew that it would be a great way to show Uman and Evelyn the difference between our plans and the plans of those who mean them no good.

"So we let the low level employee build his false food restaurant. Then my father warned Uman never to go to that evil eatery halfway up the hill. We even labeled the place SOUL FOOLED and placed the lions Curse and Consequence outside of it. The lions were to keep Uman and Evelyn out of that cursed café. I gave the owner of that poisonous place control over nothing except a large but limited amount of links to add to the lion's chains. This was simply to keep him busy while I conducted my business from the top of the hill. He never understood that each link he added only gave the lions more *freedom to pressure and pursue him. We knew that he would only use those links to try and find ways to deceive and destroy others, so we warned that unemployed builder of the nothing-which-destroys-everything that he would severely suffer for an extra eternity for every link he added to the lion's chains."*

Tru-man knew that if he didn't stop himself, he would keep writing all night until the sun came up. But he needed to be fresh and alert for the next day. He closed his pad for the night and walked toward the darkness, feeling his way back to his dugout.

He had been sleeping for about two hours when he began dreaming of the joys and delights waiting for him at the top of the hill. But suddenly, his dream shifted from the hilltop to the SOUL FOOLED restaurant with Curse and Consequence being held by the owner. The lions were roaring but the sounds they made were not lion sounds. Rather, a strange, loud buzzing came from their massive throats. Tru-man was suddenly shaken awake by Pitman. But even though he was no longer asleep, he still heard the loud buzzing from his dream. He struggled to focus on Pitman who alerted him that men from the city were nearby, cutting down the trees.

Tru-man forced himself to full consciousness, grabbed his writing pad and whatever else he could, and then quickly left his lowly lodge. He looked around and saw Angelique doing the same. The young leader screamed for everyone to run to the west. The entire Free-hand community, leaving behind most of their belongings, took off running through the woods. After about three miles the group began to slow down and look for places to rest and hide. Tru-man, catching his breath, looked at Cartman and nodded saying, "This is what Kakei was talking about. The city is probably using the tree-felling company to destroy the woods so that we have no place to hide." Several people in the group complained asking, "You knew this was gonna happen and you didn't warn us? Whose side are you on?" "Look!" Tru-man screamed. "I'm out here, out of breath, running just like you. We got a very unclear message from Kakei about this morning but didn't want to alarm anyone unnecessarily, especially if we weren't going to be able to properly tell you how to prepare for whatever was coming."

No one seemed happy with his response, or with him, for that matter. Then Angelique, who knew nothing about the message from Kakei, stepped up and offered, "You all are right to be angry." Tru-man looked at her in disbelief, wondering if he had lost her support as well. She continued, "We should have told you what we knew. We heard that something serious was going to happen this morning. Had we told you that much, you could have at least, been ready to run instead of having to leave behind many of your precious possessions. Please forgive us." After a short, tense silence someone shouted, "Just keep us in the loop next time." Another voice came, "I was just about to eat . . . I'm just sayin', y'all owe me breakfast." Tru-man cautiously smiled a relieved smile. Angelique touched his arm as she walked past and commented, "See, you don't just want me; you need me." An older gentleman, who had surprisingly outrun most of the group, came to Tru-man and confirmed Angelique's teasing critique, "That girl is good for you. You better lock that down son."

Tru-man laughed and then realized that he needed to catch up with the old-timer. "Wait a second sir. You got a minute?" he asked. "No, sorry son," the older man said, "I've got an important meeting across town." He looked Tru-man in the face with the most serious expression, and then let out a joyous laugh. "Of course son, I live in the woods. I got all the time in the world." Tru-man smiled and asked the man, "What's your name?" "Professor Wiseman," he said. "But you can call me Professor Wise." Tru-man asked, "Okay Professor Wise, let's say I wanted to 'lock that down,' how would I even do that here in the woods. It's not like we can get married. And even if we could, would that even be smart when we're living like this?"

The elder thought for a second as he took off his shoes and then said, "In light of this present danger, maybe it's not wise. It seems you're becoming something of a leader of a people in great distress. It's going to be difficult to care for the people and your wife's concerns at the same time. But, if she joins you on the mission and cares for the people like you do, and desires to aid you while you serve the common good, that just might work. If your marriage doesn't have to look like marriage did when we were back in the city where everything was hunky-dory, you just might have something. And, I think, if you find yourselves wanting to become one, and it's distracting you from the mission, then you probably need to go ahead and lock it down.

"As for how you're gonna get married out here in the woods," he paused for a moment to rub his aged and aching feet with his free hand, "Well, before I was Professor Wiseman, I was Minister Wiseman over the city's family affairs, so I suppose I could perform the ceremony. The city may not recognize my authority anymore, but I'm sure Newman and his father would approve. If I remember correctly, it's Newman's city anyway."

Tru-man's whole world suddenly seemed brighter. He smiled and said, "Then I just have one question for you." "What's that?" Minister Wiseman asked, believing he already knew what the question would be. Tru-man looked at him with a very serious face and asked, "Did you just use the phrase 'hunky-dory'?" He laughed out loud, waiting for Minister Wiseman to join him in his elation. And he did.

Tru-man called together the scouts. With Cartman at the head, he gave him his connector and then commissioned them to go into the city to see what they could find out about the plan to cut down the woods. "Tell Kakei that we've moved further west," he told Cartman. "Also, she said she had inside information. Those guys who came out this morning work for the tree-felling and processing plant. I used to work there. See if she can get any more information or tell us who her source is. Lastly, try to find out how guarded the entrance is to go up the hill. We've got to try to get a message to Newman or find out how long it will be before he comes down to the city."

Before he let them leave, he pulled Cartman to the side and whispered something in his ear. Cartman smiled and then left with the other three scouts. The remaining Free-hands once again got busy with the work of foraging for things that would help them prepare their food and build their dug-ins and hideouts. Tru-man began to work on his new abode but after a while, he stopped and called out to Angelique. He told her that he would build her shelter so that she could go and help those searching for supplies. She thanked him and took off to go join the others. Excited about his future plans, Tru-man worked hard on building his new hideout. He couldn't stop digging. He made the space twice as big as the last one, and twice as nice. When he finished, he went and helped Minister Wiseman with his hideout. Before he knew it, it was beginning to get dark. The scouts had finally made it back and some of the foraging party was beginning to return as well.

Cartman called Tru-man over and handed him back his connector and something else from his closed fist. Then Cartman began to broadcast his news. "Looks like it's about to get harder for people to go up the hill. Instead of just having guards stationed there, they're building a food court right at the bottom of the hill. It's still going to be a Halfway's-house but all different kinds of food will be served there; just no soul's food. If people insist on having soul's food, they will be given very distinct directions to that rotten restaurant halfway up the hill. Also, more trees have been cut down and more N.I.N.T.E. carvings left over top of our F-H-F marks.

Some just have the number 90 carved in them. I suspect those trees will be coming down soon. Now, are y'all sure you want all the news from the city?" Cartman paused and looked at Tru-man. Wiseman counseled, "Look son, you saw what happened this morning. No more secrets."

Cartman hung his head low and belted out, "There's a new law in the city. All Free-hand people must register as enemies of the city and spend the rest of their lives under twenty-four hour surveillance. Free-hand people cannot meet together in any unsupervised capacity. Not even husbands and wives. Anyone who mentions Newman's name can be arrested. Anyone who attempts to send a message concerning Newman will be arrested. Anyone 'sympathizers' caught trying to help a Free-handed person escape the city or evade the authorities will be arrested. Anyone who provides information leading to the arrest of an unregistered Free-hand will be rewarded. And, as of today, any Free-hand who has not registered with the city can be immediately addressed as an enemy. They will be arrested and if they resist, they will be brought down here to Gehenna and thrown into the great fire that burns continually. The city, they say, will no longer tolerate treason."

Some of the Free-hands standing around fell silently to their knees. Others cried out, "We can never go home." Some questioned, "What has Newman done to us?" Cartman turned to Tru-man and told him, "Kakei said she's got a meeting with her inside connection tonight. She should be able to tell us more tomorrow." One of the other Free-hands cried out, "You're still keeping secrets. What are you two whispering about over there?" Cartman responded, "I'm sorry. It's nothing. I'm just telling him that Kakei will meet her inside connect tonight."

The man hollered back, "Are you sure you're not over there making some kind of deal to turn us all in just so you can save yourselves?" Just then, several of the women came back from foraging and reported, "We almost didn't make it back. It got dark on us and we weren't sure which way to go. And we thought we saw men coming toward us from the city." "Where's Angelique?" Tru-man asked. But no one knew. One of them explained, "We were getting frantic. Pitman was leading us when we realized we might be lost. It turned out that we were on the right track but at some point, someone shouted out that they saw men from the city. Then everyone took off in different directions.

Upon hearing this, Tru-man dropped his connector and took off in the direction the women had just come from. Those in the crowd demanding answers from Tru-man became irate. "Where do you think you're going?" they screamed. But Tru-man had no time for their inquisition. Minister Wiseman stepped in, "Let the boy alone, he didn't ask for this responsibility, you know." The man who seemed to be leading the protest shouted at Cartman, "What did you give him? I saw you give him something secretly before you started telling us what happened in the city. No more secrets!" Wiseman answered for him, "It was an engagement link. Tru-man was going to propose to the girl when she returned."

The growing mob fell silent. They wondered if they should follow Tru-man now to help him look for Angelique. But none of them did. Not because they did not care. But because by then it was dark and they could not travel north, away from the fires of Gehenna. They could only travel back east, along the edge of the woods, toward where they had been camping previously, where men were chopping down trees not too long ago. But Cartman picked up a long tree branch and ran toward the great fire that burns continually. He lit the branch and came back to the camp. "I'm going to help him," he said. He picked up a few things from just outside of Tru-man's newly built shelter and left the camp. "I'll come with," Wiseman added. And so, they left traveling northeast, calling after Tru-man, not too loud, but not entirely too soft.

After about ten minutes of stumbling through the woods, they heard Tru-man call out to them, "Don't be afraid, it's me." He came through the bushes and joined them. "I don't know what I'm going to do. I don't know where she is," he confessed. "Don't worry. We'll help you look," they assured him. And so, the three men went walking for hours, looking for Angelique. It was after midnight when they finally came to rest as Minister Wiseman could hike no more. He sat and soothed his sore feet but Tru-man could not calm down. Wiseman told him, "I'm not trying to be insensitive son; we're gonna find her but you need to rest. Get your mind off of her just for a little while. You're just gonna keep thinking of worse and worse things. Don't you have anything to distract your mind?" "No," he said. "There's nothing strong enough to do that now."

Then Cartman supplied, "What about your book? You could write." But Tru-man remembered that he had left his book back at the camp. "I don't have it," he sighed. "Yeah, but I do," Cartman replied. He pulled it from his backpack and handed it to Tru-man who smiled, remembering how handy it had always been to have Cartman around. In his heart, Tru-man asked Angelique for permission to stop thinking of her for a little while, promising her that he was not giving up on his search. Then he took the branch lit by the great fire which burns continually and propped it up so that it hung like a lamppost. Sitting on the ground beneath it, he shook his head and chuckled. "What is it?" Wisman asked. Tru-man looked up and marveled, "I can't believe that I'm writing a book about that heavenly hill, lit by the fires of Gehenna." He opened his pad and began again to write.

> *As we approached the top of the great hill, we were greeted by so many smiling, welcoming faces and warm hugs. Unlike the SOUL FOOLED restaurant down below, Newman's establishment was full of customers. Aside from those already inside, there were six others who arrived at Newman's restaurant at the exact same moment as me. Later, while talking to one another, we discovered that each of us believed that we had been personally and privately escorted to the restaurant by Newman. And yet, somehow, not one of us was aware of the others as we ascended the hill. We each recalled traveling with Newman and him only, while having very intimate discussions with no one else around.*

How Newman accomplished this, I still do not know.

Before taking our seats, we were stopped at the counter just before the dining area and informed that the restaurant had a very strict dress code. None of us had a change of clothes and the clothes hanging up behind the attendant looked very similar to what we were already wearing. "Do we have to put on that?" I asked, pointing at the dingy clothes behind him. "Oh no," the attendant laughed. "Those articles of clothing belong to other customers who, like you, were improperly outfitted. Newman will provide something better. Will you be changed?" he asked. "Yes," we each replied. Instantly our own clothes were hanging up behind him. This caused us each a great deal of shock as, feeling totally exposed, we looked down to see whether or not we should be embarrassed. But to our surprise, we were each clothed in brilliant spectrums of light. The attendant extended his hand and announced, "Now, you may enter."

As we went into the dining area, there appeared to be only one seat left open at the long table. We looked at one another to see which one of us was more worthy of the vacant chair. But we each remembered from our conversations with Newman that the one who was seemingly least among us was the one who should have it. Just then, seven new empty seats appeared. We were relieved not to have to settle the issue ourselves. But something puzzled me: there were seven of us, and there was already one empty chair. It seemed that six more chairs would have been enough. As we sat down, I asked the guest beside me why seven more chairs were made available. She informed me that, at Newman's table, until he returns to the city, there will always be an extra chair. Or, in her words, "There's always room for one more guest."

Next came the food. We did not order anything. It became clear that the menus were not to be used in the restaurant, but only down in the city as a way to satiate us until we could reach this table. And what a table it was. But how to describe the experience? There is nothing in the city to compare to it. When the food was set before us, we learned from the other guests that we should wait, and bow. I thought, perhaps, that maybe someone would say something to give thanks for the food. But instead, something bizarre occurred. There was no audible voice, but vibrations could be felt coming from the food; it was as if the food desired us as much as we desired it. And somehow, without using words, the food was asking or thanking Newman for the opportunity to bless us. He consented, and then, we ate.

At my first bite, I felt as if my taste buds had come to life for the first time. Never before had flavor brought tears to my eyes. The food looked great in the menu. But it was twice as good in real life as it appeared to be in those pages. Every bite filled us up so that we could eat no more. But we could regain our appetite for more food simply by complimenting the chef or giving thanks to Newman who was seated at the head of the table. Once the main course was done, we were told that we must consume the utensils with which we had eaten our meals, and that, we could not use the same ones again. Each time a new meal was brought out, we were given new utensils which were always just the right size for the meals, which kept getting bigger.

All of us newcomers to Newman's table were thinking the same thing—the food went in, now something's gonna have to come out. As wonderful as the food was, there still must be some kind of excretion or gas or something. But there was not. Every single morsel of the food we ate was completely useful to our bodies so there was no waste to excrete. The only reaction our bodies had in response to the food is what physically appeared to be a yawn. The only difference was that, instead of tired air, from our windpipes came involuntary, beautiful song. It felt as if the bread we ate was still living inside of us, and still giving thanks to Newman. This made me wonder, if this food is still alive and active within me, then what happens when I eat the fast food in the city? Is it still active within me? And if so, what is it doing?

Then, Newman began to speak. I do not know if others were hearing the story for the first time or for the one-hundred-and-first time, or if, perhaps, they heard a different conversation all together, but to my ears, Newman began to complete the story that he began telling me on the way up the hill. He said to us, or to me:

"The owner of that false food establishment was ambitious, and cunning. I warned Uman and Evelyn not to go into the restaurant halfway up the hill because of Curse and Consequence. I told them that I would bring the good things out of the mall without any of the harm intended by the owner of Soul Fooled. But the builder of that place tricked them into joining him there."

Tru-man stopped writing at that moment. He heard something in the bushes and looked to Cartman and Wiseman who were sleeping just a few yards away. If something happened to them, Tru-man thought to himself, it would be his fault for keeping the fire-lit-branch burning and drawing attention to their campsite. Just then, a body lunged through the bushes. "Tru-man, I'm so glad I've found you. You've gotta go, quick!" It was Pitman. Tru-man jumped up and whispered as loud as he could, "Pitman, what happen? Where's . . ." But Pitman could not allow him to finish his question. He cut Tru-man off with, "I can't find my wife. And that girl, the one who's been helping you. She's been arrested and brought down to Gehenna to be thrown into the fire."

Wiseman and Cartman began to wake. Upon seeing Pitman they shot up to ask him, "Is Angelique with you?" "No," Tru-man answered for him. He turned to Pitman and asked, "Do you know where along Gehenna this is gonna to happen?" Pitman began to run back west toward the last campsite the Free-hands were building; he looked back and said, "Back east, just a little ways from here." Tru-man started heading southeast. Passing Wiseman and Cartman he said, "They're going to throw her into the fire. I've got to save her." Cartman grabbed the branch lit by the great fire and handed it to Wiseman, "Go back to the camp," he told him, "I'm gonna go with Tru-man." Wiseman took the branch and pulled Cartman close to tell him, "Don't let him do anything foolish. He may be in love, but the people need him to live." Cartman nodded his head and then took off after Tru-man.

As they ran along the edge of the wood, their path partially lit by the great fire across from them, they saw a crowd gathered ahead of them. The closer they got, they began to hear what sounded like someone giving a speech. They climbed up into the woods and continued to get close enough to see and hear what was happening in the crowd. As they got closer, they heard a distinct voice say, ". . . if you just come out. You can save your friends. They will not be harmed if those of you hiding out in the woods would just give yourselves up. This is a promise from the city's leaders. No one will harm you. These eight Free-hands and these two Free-hand sympathizers standing here, along with every one of you will be escorted back to town and live under supervision. But if you do not come out, your friends standing here, who have been found guilty of treason will be marched into the great fire."

Tru-man thought out loud, "How long do we have before they start forcing people into the flames?" Cartman stood silent. Then, the crowd began to move west along the outskirts of the great fire that burns continually. Tru-man and Cartman followed the crowd from within the woods. After about one-hundred yards, the crowd stopped. Then the man with the distinct voice repeated his speech concerning what would happen if the Free-hands in the woods gave themselves up. But this time he added, "For every one of you that comes out, I will let one of these Free-hands live. If five of you come out, I will let you choose five of these Free-hands standing here to return with you to the city." Tru-man waited thinking of all the options and trying to spot Angelique in the crowd. After five more minutes the crowd turned to move west again. Just then, Tru-man spotted the only face in the crowd he recognized. It was the woman who had been helping him, but not Angelique. It was Kakei. Cartman also recognized her from corresponding with her on Tru-man's connector.

Tru-man regretted out loud that he did not have his connector with him. "Maybe," he thought, "she tried to warn us or tell us that the city was on to her. I need my connector." "I got you covered," Cartman informed him as he reached into his backpack and pulled out the device. "Is there anything you don't have when I need it?" Tru-man asked with a smile. Cartman handed it to him but questioned, "If you turn it on, won't it tell them where we are?" "Yes," he said, "but it's a risk I have to take. Kakei risked her life to help us. She may have left us valuable information. We'll turn it right back off and move to another spot just as soon as we read her most recent post." And that is what they did.

On Kakei's dot display page, there was a new posting that read, *"Please Help! Tonight, I'm in the hot seat because of all my help to you. If you choose to stay hidden, I will not single you out. But, I hope you will come to pick me out of the crowd."*

The crowd was moving again. Tru-man and Cartman knew it would not be long before the crowd got close enough for the Free-hand campsite to hear them. Just then, three members of the Free-hand-fellowship came out from the woods to surrender, one of whom was Minister Wiseman. The eight captured Free-hands and two captured Free-hand sympathizers (one of whom was Kakei) rejoiced.

The crowd who was there to watch the executions called for more Free-hands to come out and rescue the others. Then two more members of the fellowship came out of the woods. Four of the five fellowship members chose a captured Free-hand to be taken back to the city with. Minister Wiseman, was about to choose Kakei as his rescued partner, but instead, decided to choose the other Free-hand sympathizer. Seeing that none of them chose to rescue Kakei, Tru-man declared, "I'm going to save her." He feared that Cartman might try to stop him but the only response he heard was a strange sounding "Shhhhhh," followed by an even stranger, "You sure about that?"

He turned and, to his surprise, saw the shadowy figure of a man standing behind Cartman with his right hand covering Cartman's mouth. From the few flashes of Gehenna's light which penetrated the dark woods, Tru-man saw a scar on the back of the hand that muted Cartman. To his shock, the scar formed the shape of the number 90. He remembered Cartman's earlier reports of the N.I.N.T.E. carvings on the trees in the city where F-H-F had been crossed out. Was this some sort of secret police formed to hunt down the Free-hand-fellowship, he wondered. But he noticed that the scarred right hand had no chain attached to it. Then, the man holding back Cartman's fearful scream marched him forward a few feet until the light from Gehenna hit his face. He stood in the light and smiled the most peaceful smile. At this, Tru-man smiled as Cartman struggled to make sense of the encounter. Tru-man elated as loudly and as safely as he could, "My Maine-man!"

Jermaine let Cartman go and stepped forward to greet Tru-man with a Free-hand shake and a hug. "Please Maine," Tru-man begged, "Tell me what in the world is going on." Jermaine began explaining, "That girl is not what she seems. Did you know that the name Kakei means Untrustworthy? I learned that from one of the Asian neighborhoods in the city. She was playing you and me both. I was her inside connection for some of the information she was feeding you. Once she realized that I was following the messages you were posting, she contacted me. I told her that I was starting a resistance group called the N.I.N.T.E. She claimed that she wanted to reconnect me with you. She wanted to know where my camp was so that she could begin telling your people to leave Gehenna and meet up with my teams. We're held up in the North Hills but I would not tell her where. She seemed to want to know too much, too soon. I was crossing out your F-H-F signs as a message to you, trying to tell you to meet us in the hills because Gehenna's not safe.

"I was only Kakei's source for inside information concerning all the bizarre things happening at the tree-felling company. And most of that stuff she hasn't even told you. The other information she gets straight from the city, from her new boss, the city controller Mr. Ruind." Tru-man cut in, "So what happens to her if I don't go down there to rescue her?" "Nothing man. She goes back to work," Jermaine answered and then added, "But I can tell you what will happen if you do go down there. Anyone who comes out of the woods, along with the Free-hands they think they're rescuing, will be thrown into fire regardless." Tru-man's eyes got wide as he thought about the lives about to be lost.

He felt foolish for trusting Kakei and for wanting to rescue her, so he asked, "When did you know she was a fraud?" Jermaine responded, "I had my suspicions but wasn't sure until today. She didn't know I was following her when she went to have lunch with Mr. Ruind. I watched as she showed him her connector and then he gave his approval about what was on it. Right after that, she posted that distress message on her dot display page. After she posted it, she and Mr. Ruind laughed and enjoyed each other for the rest of the afternoon. That message was posted for you and me to see so that one or both of us would come down here tonight and try to save her by turning ourselves in. I knew I had to come here just in case you tried to rescue her. I didn't know how I was going to find you but then, just moments ago, your connector turned on and I saw that you were less than a mile away from me. So I ran this way and here you are."

Tru-man had many questions. "You could detect me, but I could not detect you?" He wondered out loud. Jermaine, understanding Tru-man's dismay, addressed him patiently, "The N.I.N.T.E. has people working in every section of the city. Some with a free hand and some with both hands still chained; they have never been up the great hill, but they hope to someday. Our people who work in the media center have scrambled a few connectors so that we cannot be detected when we use them. We still cannot send out messages about Newman. But we do what we can."

Just then, Cartman interrupted them, "They're pushing them in!" Tru-man and Jermaine ran to the opening in the bushes and looked with horror as one by one, captured and surrendered Free-hands, along with the one true captured sympathizer, were forced into the flames. Kakei, however, was not offered to the great fire which burns continually. The crowd cheered and began to chant anti-Newman slogans. Feeling utterly helpless and defeated, Tru-man and Jermaine looked down and then started to turn away, but Cartman called them back. "Look!" he screamed. As they turned back and gazed into Gehenna, they could not believe their eyes.

The men had pushed fourteen people into the fire but there came quickly a fifteenth figure walking through the flames to meet them. He touched each one of them and as he did so, they ceased suffering. A table appeared and they all sat down amidst the dancing tongues of fire. And then, most amazingly, they began to enjoy a meal right there in the blaze, right in front of their enemies. When Cartman recognized that it was indeed Newman who had met his friends in the flames, he jumped from the bushes and ran past the astonished crowd and leaped into the great fire. As he entered, a chair appeared at the table and all of the martyred guests welcomed him.

Those in the crowd, who were recording the execution on their connectors, could not believe their eyes. Some of them, after seeing what happened for Cartman, decided that they too would barge in upon the flaming festivities, certain that a place would be made at the table for them as well. They looked around and told their friends to keep recording as they stepped into the great fire. As they entered, they remained unharmed. That is, until Newman turned and looked at them with the most unwelcoming stare, as if they had rudely intruded upon a private party. Instantly, Newman and his guests were gone. The table violently burst into flames and the men who entered uninvited did the same. The man with the distinct voice told the city agents standing nearby to confiscate the connectors of those who had recorded the event. But several of them sent the recording out to friends before the agents could take their devices away.

It thrilled Tru-man to see that Newman was not unaware of what was happening in the city. He remembered the last thing Newman said to him before he left the hill, "Know that I will always be with you, even if you are all the way at the other end of the city." He thought to himself that if Newman was able to protect his friends from the fires of Gehenna, then he could certainly be trusted to take care of Angelique, wherever she was. This gave him much comfort.

Just then, Pitman and a few other fellowship members stumbled upon them. "I still can't find my wife," he said. "But we can't go back west. It's crawling with city agents back there." Tru-man turned to Jermaine and suggested, "Your N.I.N.T.E. could use a couple more free hands, couldn't it?" "There's always room for one more guest," Jermaine affirmed with a smile. Then he added, "It's gonna take us a while to get to the North Hills. I have some business in the city. Plus we can only travel in between the city agent's patrol times so we'll have to remain pretty well hidden and blend into the city at certain points." "Cool," Tru-man said, accepting the mission on behalf of the remaining Free-hand-fellowship. He then turned to Pitman and offered whatever comfort he could concerning his missing wife. He told him how Newman had just protected his friends in the fire. This helped, but only a little, since Pitman had never met Newman personally.

Then Tru-man turned to Jermaine and said, "A minute ago you mentioned some pretty bizarre things happening at the tree-felling company. Why don't you put us down with all that?" That seemed like a good way to pass the time, so Jermaine positioned himself in the middle of the pack and began to bring them up to speed concerning the plot of the media company, the tree fellers, the city controller, and the new ambassador and, soon to be, Supreme Head of Nameless City, Mr. Screwtape.

The Book of Trumaine

After a week of traveling, hiding and meeting with other Free-hands in the city, Tru-man, Pitman and the six other remaining members of the Free-hand-fellowship arrived at the North Hills with Jermaine. As they approached the foot of the hills, many members of the N.I.N.T.E. came out to welcome them. But two young women, more than the rest, came eagerly climbing down to meet them. One of them was Angelique, who had escaped city agents days ago and traveled north until she spotted other Free-hands on their way to the North Hills. Tru-man's eyes locked on her as he ran to her and held her tight.

He was so focused on his love that he did not even notice that the other young woman was his sister Imani, whose name means faith. Her name had proven to be fitting in that she had not been to the top of the great hill, to Newman's table, and yet she believed in the things she heard from Tru-man and others ever since she read his menu that night many months ago. She was glad to see her brother, but she did not just climb down the hill to meet him. Since Tru-man first went missing, she had been faithfully following the messages being posted on his dot display page and then noticed that Jermaine was doing the same thing. The two of them eventually met and fell in love during the months since her brother had gone to live in the woods near Gehenna.

When Tru-man finished embracing Angelique, he turned to introduce her to Jermaine but saw Jermaine embracing Imani. Confused at first, he quickly realized the situation and saw it as a cause for more celebration. They all hugged one another then Jermaine, jokingly turned to Tru-man and announced, "I'd like to introduce you to my PRE-ancé, Imani." Tru-man laughed, but had to stop to ask about the term PRE-ancé. Imani informed him that the word was indeed what it sounded like, the combination of "pre" and "fiancé." She told him that in the hills, they had chosen to do away with the terms "boyfriend and girlfriend." When asked why, Jermaine explained that they had observed how, down in the city, those titles were often treated as more official than they really were—leading couples to act as if they had rights to one another's time and body in a way that was really more fit for marriage. Instead of using terms that focused on and celebrated the temporary status of a couple's relationship, they created a new term that would keep couples focused on the future, more permanent relationship they hoped to have; while at the same time, reminding them of what they were not yet and the rights they did not yet have.

Tru-man nodded, approving of the new logic. Then, Imani turned to Angelique, whom she had been hanging out with for the last couple of days, and asked Tru-man, "And I presume this is your PRE-ancé, Angelique?" Everyone laughed. But Tru-man shook his head and said, "No." The laughter stopped as he got down on both knees and pulled out a small link from a chain, he put it on around the two middle fingers of Angelique's right hand. Then he bowed his head and waited to see if she would take it off. This was the engagement custom in

Nameless City. She did not remove it. Instead, she leaned over and touched her forehead to his, accepting his marriage proposal. The whole community cheered and began to celebrate.

Seizing the moment, Jermaine quieted the crowd. He turned to Tru-man and Angelique and said, "You kind of stole my thunder but, oh well." Then he got down on his knees and pulled out the link he had been holding for several weeks, waiting for the right time to propose marriage to Imani. The community erupted into song and celebration again as she leaned forward and accepted his proposal. This had a therapeutic effect on the new hillside society. The idea of marriage helped them to feel as though life could go on with some hope for normalcy. Down in the Nameless City, marriages were to take place exactly two weeks from the hour of engagement. The N.I.N.T.E. decided to keep this tradition alive and so, the women set about preparing for the double wedding. They understood however, that the men, especially these two men, could not perform their traditional duties in the next two weeks. And so they exempted Tru-man and Jermaine as it would be their job to work on forging the future of the new community.

After five days of meeting and planning, Tru-man and Jermaine called a meeting to discuss the plans of the N.I.N.T.E. Seventy-five of the three-hundred people living in the North Hills (some with a free hand, others still chained) showed up. Many of the others sent word saying, "Just tell us what you need us to do and we'll do it." And so, the meeting began with Jermaine recapping the situation.

"So, here's what we know. The city says that it has been taking temperature readings over the last twenty years and now believes that, unless something changes, over the next fifty years the city is going to get colder and colder until the temperature reaches below freezing and remains that way all year around. They say that within the next seventy-five years, the air will become unbearably cold and that this will lead to the death and extinction of Nameless City. To combat this cold, they say they will cut down as many trees as necessary so that the city will have wood to burn for heat when the city begins to freeze.

"We believe that this is a lie and just another part of a fourfold attack against Newman and those of us who know him. The first angle of attack was to distract and discourage people from going up the great hill. They did this with the new food-court that blocks the way up. If anyone makes it to the hill beyond it, they are severely detoured by very clear directions leading them to that false food restaurant located only halfway up. The next level of attack was against us. They wanted to get all friends of Newman under constant supervision or, if possible, out of the city and if necessary, into Gehenna.

"Then there's the issue of the connectors. Everyone here has experienced getting shutdown and blacked-out when trying to communicate Newman's name. We learned from our friends in the media center that there has been a deliberate attempt over the last ten years to get everyone using connectors; not just so that all information in the entire city could be digitally documented and accessible to all. But the reason they made connectors available for everyone was so that any message communicated to the masses could be monitored and controlled. This leads to the fourth angle of attack. We have it on good authority from our friends at the tree-felling company that the real reason behind the cutting down of the trees is to eliminate the production of paper in order to stop Free-hands and Free-hand sympathizers from writing and spreading the word about Newman the old fashion way, now that we cannot use our connectors to do it.

"So, our response will be fourfold. We have crews working around the clock on digging tunnels, beginning at various points around the city, which will lead to the great hill behind the food-court but before the Chain Exchange gate. Next we have engaged in learning the paper making process. Through our connections at the tree-felling company, we will get enough wood to practice on and produce our own paper. At the same time, we are requesting that each person here put the story of their encounter with Newman in writing. We will collect ninety stories and bind them into one book. And then we will copy that book to produce as many as we possibly can in order to distribute them in the city, even if we must risk our lives to do it. And the fourth level of our response, I'll let Tru-man explain."

Tru-man stood up and began, "All of you here know that we have several connectors that can transmit without being located. But you can't transmit Newman's name. I have a connector that can transmit Newman's name, but can also be tracked and located. We now know that none of our friends in the media center can alter a device to be able to transmit Newman's name. That ability has to come from the City Center. Therefore, we need to take my connector and combine it with the technology in your connectors which allows you to not be traced. I wish we could give my connector to our friends in the media center to have them add the cloaking ability to it, but we can't risk losing the only connector that can transmit our story to the entire city at one time. And so, we will create a technology lab here in the hills in order to work on combining these capabilities. Once we succeed, we will scan in the stories written by the community and transmit them digitally. That's it. I'll pass it back to my Maine-man."

Jermaine stepped back into the helm and added, "When each of you came to the North Hills, you filled out a form which asked you to list your natural talents and strengths as well as your skills and any training you've received. Many of you have also mentioned feeling energized in some particular way by that mysterious presence, that alluring aroma which radiates from your menus. So if you feel empowered to serve our community in a different way than what your natural skills and talents suggest please let us know. Otherwise, based on what we know about you, we will assign you to one of the four missions previously mentioned. That's about it. Are there any questions?"

"I've got a question," someone shouted. "Is it true that Newman showed up in the fires of Gehenna?" Another shouted, "Why don't we just head down to the south end of the city now and meet Newman in the flames?" But Tru-man shouted, "That's suicide. There's no guarantee that Newman will meet you there just because you decided to throw yourself in." But the questioner responded, "It's a good thing Newman showed up when your people were there. If it weren't for him, how many of your people would have been killed all because you trusted that treacherous woman?" The assembly began to turn against Tru-man. Pitman, who was standing beside him, was not in favor of the seeming suicide mission. After all, he had not been to the top of the hill to meet Newman, and he missed Newman's firework display at Gehenna. On top of that, his wife was still missing and he had hopes of seeing her again.

At that point, Jermaine stepped in with, "Listen! When the city turned against us, there were only two men who stood to organize against them and help our persecuted brothers and sisters—myself, and this man here. For that reason alone, he deserves a little more respect from us all. And I myself was almost fooled by the same woman!" But a voice shouted, "Yeah but you weren't, that's why we're following you. Now take us to Newman!"

Jermaine stopped and thought for a second, and then asked them, "How many of you believe that you have been gifted in some particular way, energized by that alluring aroma that radiates from our menus, to serve this community and those in the city who may become a part of this community?" Almost everyone in the meeting who had been up the great hill raised their free hand. Jermaine continued, "Do you think that you would have been gifted and energized to serve others in such a way if Newman's plan was for all of you to make such a self-centered decision?

"Now, if you suddenly find yourself in a situation where your life is in danger, it may be that you will meet Newman again sooner than you expected. But until then you are here, not for your own sake, but for the sake of others who will benefit from your gifts, talents, skills and energy. In other words, stop thinking about yourselves. We are doing this so that our chained and emaciated brothers and sisters in the city can come to know the emancipating goodness of Newman's table."

The crowd remained silent, but could not remain in the cavern where the meeting took place. Jermaine's words were echoing off the walls too much for that. But even as they left, his words still echoed in the inner chambers of their hearts and minds. Tru-man turned to him with a look of gratitude, mixed with a bit of surprise, and uttered his now famous phrase, "My Maine-man." The two friends laughed. "When did you become such an orator, such a leader?" he asked. Jermaine responded, "I don't know man, ever since I came back down the hill, it's been that way. I guess that's my mysterious gift from Newman."

Tru-man confessed, "I'm not that much of a leader. I don't know what I've been gifted to do." But Jermaine encouraged him, "Yo, I hope you don't mind man, but I took a look at the account you've been writing about your trip up the hill. I've heard other people try to tell their story, but the way you write . . . that might be what you're gifted to do man. In fact, why don't take charge of the writing project?" But Tru-man questioned humbly, "Are you sure Maine-man? That's a very important undertaking. Plus, I thought maybe I would oversee the connector project."

"Nah man," Jermaine maintained, "You're not a scientist or a technician or an engineer. You, my friend, are a literary beast! Do that. Plus, we're gonna need someone who's paid very close attention to detail while they were on the hill to oversee the project; to authenticate and synchronize all the submissions we're gonna get. Feel me?" And Tru-man did. He nodded in agreement. Sensing the significance of the job before him, he felt the nervous excitement beginning to rise within him. It was almost too much. A new mission giving him a sense of purpose; a fiancé to look forward to—life in the

North Hills with Newman's friends was better than life in the city had ever been, even with all of its modern conveniences.

"What about me?" Pitman asked. Jermaine looked at Tru-man as if to say, "That's up to you." Tru-man proposed, "Why don't you help with the tunnels and lead the crews down into the city?" "Or," Pitman countered, "I can stay up here with y'all and help run things." But Tru-man, trying to lead like Jermaine had just done with the large crowd, said, "Well think about it; you know the city. Our people are going to be at risk down there and you still have both of your hands chained. As their foreman, you can help them blend in and keep people from asking questions about the tunnels." After going back and forth, Pitman finally agreed and then left the meeting, feeling just slightly jealous of how Tru-man's new life seemed to be working out more than his own.

Pitman missed his wife all the more now. He went to the cavern where the connectors were stored in order to reach out to her. The N.I.N.T.E. had arranged a system whereby anyone could come and use a connector to send messages to people in the city without being tracked by the city. The only condition was that all messages had to be approved before being sent. This was to make sure that the sender was not jeopardizing the safety of the community by giving away their location. Every day, once in the morning and once at night, Pitman would go and post a message hoping that his wife would see it and respond. But on this day, feeling a little upset by the way the meeting had just ended for him, Pitman had a bit of a chip on his shoulder.

He began composing his message to his wife, but when the Free-hand who was guarding the connectors began to oversee Pitman's message, Pitman snapped. "C'mon man! You see me walkin' around here with Tru-man and Maine-man every day. Do you look over their shoulders when they're sending messages? No! And why are we screening people's conversations? How does that make us any different than the people down in the city we're hiding from? I mean, ain't that how they started cracking down on the Free-hands in the first place? Gimmie some space to say something to my wife!" Everyone was aware of Pitman's family situation and had sympathy for him, knowing that he had not yet been to Newman's table. From that day forward, he never had to ask for privacy when using the connectors again. This, he felt, was a start at getting some of the same respect that came along with Tru-man's new life. But down in the city, plans would soon be made to bring Tru-man's sweet life in the hills to a bitter end.

Kakei was moving up in the ranks at her City Center job. She had become Mr. Ruind's right hand woman. As such, she accompanied him to a meeting with the heads of the new leading industries. As the two of them entered the building, Mr. Ruind told her that she was being invited as his guest. He mainly wanted to impress her by looking important with the other men. He, therefore, reminded her that she was not to speak and that she had no agenda in the meeting. She agreed that she was only there to witness the "big men" at work and offer whatever kind of support he needed. This, of course, made him feel all the more like the big man he wanted to be.

As they entered the conference room, she saw Mr. Taskman from the tree-felling company, Mr. Conman from the media company, and Mr. Screwtape, the new ambassador from the Chain Linked Nation. No one in the Nameless City knew exactly what or where the Chain Linked Nation was. But, as far back as anyone could remember, Mr. Screwtape's realm had been responsible for chaining the hands and neck of every citizen in Nameless City sometime between birth and the age of twelve years old. This was based on an ancient agreement with Newman that, whenever someone was born with the images of Curse and Consequence on their hands, that person could be bound in chains. The images of the lions could only be seen on the hill, or by those who were not natural born descendants of Uman and Evelyn. In all of history, there had only ever been one human who did not bear those marks and whom the Chain Linked Nation was not able to bind.

Every so often, the Nation would send an ambassador to Nameless City in order to attempt to make an accord with the city's leaders. Mr. Screwtape was the newest ambassador who offered Mr. Ruind a new deal. He would break the Chain Linked Nation's agreement with Newman and no longer bind the hands and necks of the children of the city if Mr. Ruind could influence a vote to make Mr. Screwtape the supreme leader of the land. Screwtape could not offer to unchain any of the adults because his realm only possessed the chains, and not the keys to the locks. At any rate, this was the closest anyone from the Nation had ever come to striking a deal with a city official. In fact, Mr. Ruind had already begun functioning under Screwtape's authority. The hard part, however, was never getting the officials to submit. Rather, it was getting the people of the city to give up their independence to the Chain Linked Nation. But, Mr. Ruind was a very persuasive and charismatic individual who knew how to motivate the city to move in the directions he chose.

Mr. Ruind sat down around the meeting table while Kakei took the initiative to sit beside him. Each of the other men had at least two women sitting behind them for two reasons—one, to take notes; and two, to make the other men at the table take note of him. As the conversation went on, Mr. Taskman asked, "What about the Free-hands in the North Hills? Have we located them yet?" "No," Mr. Ruind responded. "But I've still got a few people on it." "Pull'em off," Mr. Screwtape said in his distinct voice. "We need more men to help get the trees down. Plus, the Free-hands can't do much harm from the hills. We'll get'em eventually; but right now the focus is on the trees."

Mr. Taskman, concerned about the future of his industry, demanded to know, "Now what about us? What about my men? Sure, business is booming now, but we'll have all of the city's trees down in a couple of years at this rate. Then, another couple of years turning the wood into products to sell, and then what? We'll be out of jobs." Screwtape corrected him, "Sooner than that." "What?" Taskman shot back. Screwtape confirmed, "It won't take any more than a couple of years to put you all out of work. We're not taking the wood and turning it into anything except smoke. You won't be able to find two specs of wood dust when we're done."

Mr. Conman, the youngest man in the room at age twenty-two, sensed the tension building and offered Taskman a solution. "When the tree jobs are all gone, your men can come work for me. I'll find them a job in the media. After all, everything is turning digital these days. The decreased demand for paper products was killing your industry anyway." But he had no intention of keeping his word. Screwtape heard and appreciated Conman's lie on his behalf. But he exposed two truths when he said, "Why thank you Mr. Conman, but Taskman's real concern is not for his workers, but for his own financial future. So you would only need to open up one job in the media to relieve the tension of this moment."

"Ah! I see," Conman said. "Well consider it done." "Thanks," Mr. Taskman mumbled. But Screwtape, looking back and forth between Kakei and the men at the table revealed, "Don't thank Mr. Conman. He was lying through his teeth with both offers." Screwtape was an expert at understanding the way people thought, their motivations and what drove them to do the things they did. Each of the men looked around the table with untrusting eyes and crooked, conniving smiles. "Don't worry Taskman," Screwtape said, "I'll make sure you're well taken care of."

While all of this was going on, Kakei was distracted by a disturbing message she received on her connector. After reading and reflecting on it for several minutes, her rage got the best of her. Screwtape sensed her fury and took a kind of evil pleasure in it as she sat brewing with poisonous passions. When she could no longer hold it in, she blurted out, "You can't take your attention off the Free-hands in the North Hills." "Shut up!" Mr. Ruind shouted at her. But she continued, "They're plotting something big! I just got an instant thought from an inside source who says that in just under ten days, the Free-hands will have amassed a stockpile of poison that they plan to sneak into the city to contaminate the fast food supply. They think this will force people to make a trip up the great hill."

"Let me see that," Taskman demanded. "It's gone. The person removed the post," she quickly explained. But Mr. Conman challenged, "You said it was an instant thought, it should be in your inbox. Shouldn't it?" "That's not what I meant," she threw back. "I have my connector set to always alert me when one of my inside sources posts something and it just alerted me to a public post. But it's gone now."

Ruind sighed, "Well now we've gotta go up there. I can't have them coming down into the city with that. The tax payers would have my head. Get the exact date and find out where they are! I'll put a team together." "Okay. I'll try my best," Kakei assured him. The other men agreed as they complimented Mr. Ruind on having such a beautiful and resourceful female in his close company. But while Mr. Screwtape outwardly agreed with the others, he inwardly and instantly knew Kakei was lying about the message. He had had years of practice learning when men and women were being motivated by something other than what they said. From that moment on, he despised Kakei. Even though he himself was a master at lying and concealing the truth from others, he passionately and hypocritically hated being lied to. From that day on, he began plotting ways to kill Kakei.

On their way out of the meeting, Screwtape instructed Mr. Ruind to, "Send that girl by my office. I can tell she's good at what she does. From now on we'll share her. She'll work part-time for you and part of the time for me." Mr. Ruind didn't know how to respond. He did not want to look weak in front of the others, or Kakei. But he knew that he could not slight or deny Mr. Screwtape in the least. Kakei smiled, feeling good about her new importance to the man who seemed to be really in charge.

Still, she figured it would be good to help Mr. Ruind save face just in case things didn't work out with Mr. Screwtape. "I'm sure he'll send me over, if he can spare me. In the meantime, I trust your girls will suffice," she said as she smiled confidently. Turning her nose up at the other women waiting by the door, she left with Mr. Ruind. Once in the elevator, he turned to her and asked, "Where did you get that information from? Who's your source?" Sensing that the power in their relationship had shifted in her favor, Kakei responded, but only with, "You know me sweetheart, I always keep an ace in the hole." They both smiled, looking at one another with suspect eyes, and then went on with their plans for the day.

In the hills, things were moving along. Every day, teams were going out disguised as city workers, digging tunnels underneath the city's surface. The writing project was going well as Tru-man had inspired many people to write, some who had had technical training and others who were simply passionate about telling their story. But the technicians were still having trouble getting the connectors to remain stealth while sending messages about Newman at the same time; they kept shutting down. Imani, who had fully given herself to the task of preparing for the upcoming double wedding, realized that Angelique seemed to be preoccupied. When she could pull the dead weight of Angelique's distracted mind no longer, she confronted her. "What's wrong girl? Don't tell me you're not really in love with my brother after all."

"No," Angelique assured her. "It's not that. It's just that everyone is pitching in to help with the mission and, if I couldn't do anything, that'd be fine. But I know that I can. I should be in the cavern with the techs working on those connectors. I'm almost certain that no one in there knows as much about them as me and I have some great ideas about what we could get them to do. But, I don't want you to feel like I'm abandoning you with all this wedding stuff." "Fine," Imani sulked. "Go ahead; be a guy. Just show up and say 'I do'." But she couldn't keep a straight face. They both laughed as Imani encouraged her, "Seriously though, you can go and help. I'll take care of everything. And I really, really do hope that you can help . . . help show those guys what a woman can do." They laughed again as Angelique quickly gathered her things and then sprinted over to the hillside gathering where the technicians were working.

After several more days, Tru-man finished his portion of the book that was to be bound. He submitted it to the committee that was created to organize and vote on all of the literary submissions. Overall, 130 written accounts were submitted by the community but after careful inspection, half of them were rejected. Many of them were not well written and were hard to understand. Some were filled with details that did not really add meaning to the story. Others seemed like the authors were reporting more of what the owner of the SOUL FOOLED restaurant told them than what was heard from Newman. And still, others sounded like they had been written by people who had not yet been up the great hill, but instead were telling what they hoped it will be like when they finally get there.

In the end, only sixty-six submissions were chosen and found to be authentic and consistent. A few of these stories were submitted anonymously. One or two were, admittedly, not firsthand accounts but stories that were told to the author by another. But when compared with other firsthand accounts, they were found to be accurate and trustworthy nonetheless. Some of the authors submitted multiple writings based on different conversations they had with Newman. The committee decided that Truman's account, labeled "The Book of Trumaine" which contained five sections, was to be first in the N.I.N.T.E.'s book.

Just as the sun was beginning to set, the community got together for a great feast. They made makeshift tables and every table had an empty place at the head of it, for Newman. They ate and sang and laughed as if there was no such thing as a city below them trying to pull them down. After the meal, Jermaine stood up and everyone shouted, "My Maine-man!" stealing Tru-man's nickname for him. They all laughed and then Jermaine began to update them on the progress of the group's missions.

"We have completed three tunnels. Two more are still in the works and should be done in a couple of days. The connector, I am pleased to inform you, has been connected! We can now send instant thoughts and post messages from Tru-man's device without being detected. And for this, we have the more than competent Ms. Angelique to thank." Everyone applauded her while Tru-man caressed and gently squeezed her hand. Angelique smiled a humble smile, hoping in her heart that Newman was pleased by her contribution.

Jermaine continued, "Thank you all for your writing submissions. The book has been completed. It has not been bound yet. First, we have to scan every page into the connector so that we can get ready to send it out to feed our starving friends and enemies down in the city. The cover of the book will read N I N T E." He spelled it out while the crowd cheered. But Tru-man tapped Jermaine at that point and informed him, "Sorry man, I don't know if you've heard. We didn't end up with ninety stories; just

sixty-six. I hope that doesn't ruin the name for you."
Jermaine laughed, "Is that what you think N.I.N.T.E.
stands for?" Seeing the confusion on Tru-man's face,
he leaned over and pronounced the true meaning of
the letters into his ear. Tru-man smiled sheepishly,
feeling foolish for distrusting the name when he first
heard of it and then for thinking it merely referred
to a set number of people or writings for the book.

Just then, one of the techs came running up the
hill, up to the place where Tru-man and Jermaine
stood. In her hand was Tru-man's connector. "You
have to see this," she shouted. "We were scanning
pages into the connector to get ready for the big
posting but then an instant thought popped up from
Kakei. But look what it says." They read it silently.
Then Tru-man looked fearfully up at Angelique.
"What?" she demanded to know. "What does it say?"
someone else in the crowd shouted. "It's from my ex-
girlfriend," Tru-man lamented. "The woman who
almost tricked us at Gehenna. She says, *'I hear
congratulations are in order. I know I'm not invited to
your wedding in a couple of days but don't worry, I'm
sending my best . . . or should I say, the city's best.'"*

A great fear fell over those who heard him
while the word spread throughout the crowd to
those who did not. Jermaine thought for a moment
and then asked, "How in the world could she have

heard about the wedding? Who here has been sending unauthorized messages to someone in the city?" But no one responded. "It seems the North Hills are now the molehills," he said in a disgusted tone. "Someone here is a spy."

Everyone looked around at the person next to him or her, trying to spot the traitor. Some people even began to question others about suspicious activity they had witnessed recently. Pitman suggested to Tru-man, "We should leave now; take Angelique and let's just bounce." But Imani shouted, "Stop it! Everyone just be quiet and stop accusing each other. There is no spy here." "How do you know?" Pitman asked. "Because," she yelled. "If the person that tipped Kakei off about the wedding is a spy, then that would mean that I am a spy."

A huge gasp came from the crowd. "Why love? Why would you do that?" Jermaine asked his bride to be. Imani explained, "When we all got engaged, I was so happy. I wanted to tell my brother down in the city that Trumaine and I were both getting married. But my brother and I never liked Kakei. We knew that she still had feelings for Trumaine and that it would bother her to learn that he was engaged to Angelique. I told my brother down in the city to make sure that Kakei hears about it. But that was right after we got engaged; before y'all told us about Kakei working for the city and trying to set you both up to get arrested at Gehenna. After that, I really wanted her to find out. It was the only way I thought we could hurt her for what she did. I never thought that she'd be able to do anything about it. I'm sorry." "From now on, every message gets screened before it's sent," Jermaine commanded. The whole community stood in silence, sensing their vulnerability to the impending danger.

Then, Tru-man shouted, "Tonight!" "What?" Imani asked. "Let's do it tonight. Let's do the weddings tonight," he said with the utmost excitement. He reasoned, "They think the wedding is in two days. We can get married tonight; finish digging at least one of the other two tunnels tomorrow; get the book scanned by tomorrow night and send it out. And we can get teams working on the manual copies of the book and try to create at least ten copies by tomorrow night." But Angelique warned, "We won't be able to edit or proofread the copies." "I know," Tru-man admitted. "The copies may have some mistakes as far as the words. But all the ideas will be right. Then, while the city is coming up here two nights from now, we will be down in the city escorting people through the tunnels; distributing the books and moving the entire N.I.N.T.E. camp to the western hills. We'll be further away from the city but we'll have much more room to hide and time to plan our next move."

Jermaine shook his head in approval and affirmed him with, "Who's the leader now?" "It's just a plan," Tru-man said humbly. "You've still gotta get the people moving on it." Tru-man was right. And so, Jermaine lifted his hands and yelled, "Would you join your hearts to ours as we celebrate our vows tonight, even as you prepare to detach your hearts from these hills tomorrow." The people drew strength from their leader and the celebration began. Imani and Angelique went to get ready. The literary council chose seventy-two people and appointed them to get started on copying the sixty-six books of the N.I.N.T.E. And Pitman made his nightly trip to use the public connector.

It was around nine o'clock when the double wedding got under way. There was no city minister and no city to sanction their vows, but the couples made their pledges to one another, to the entire N.I.N.T.E. society and to the highest power they could think of, situated upon the top of the great hill. Songs ensued and as the festivities continued, the couples walked through the celebration to their private caves where they would be able to creatively speak their vows to one another again using all the languages of love.

The celebration died down and the night tried to end but, it could not. As Tru-man lay next to his new wife, he tried to dream but a distressing sound kept annoying him. Finally, he awoke to hear clearly what disturbed his dreams. "They're coming! Wake up! Wake Up!" a voice screamed. Tru-man shot up and shook Angelique awake. They ran to the mouth of their cave and saw countless lights moving up the hill toward them. "Go and get Imani," Tru-man told his soul's mate. "Where are you going?" she asked. "I'm going to send the book out to everyone in the city, however much of it has been scanned in. Meet me where the connectors are." They ran their separate ways and that was the last time he saw Angelique on this side of the great hill.

As he arrived at the tech center he found the place in complete disarray. Pages had been strewn everywhere as the copiers ran in fright. But there were two bundled stacks of papers that had been undisturbed in the panic. One, the larger stack, was all of the original pages submitted by the N.I.N.T.E. community; and the other, shorter stack was a complete copy of only the sixty-six accounts selected for binding. He ran over to inspect his connector and found that all sixty-six accounts had been scanned in. Chaos was collecting outside the cave but he took as much time as he could to select a massive amount of people to alert to the posting of the digital book.

He thought of Newman kindly in his heart and asked him to deliver the message to all the right recipients, ones who would respond favorably to the reports of Newman's friends. And then, he posted it.

Just then, Jermaine came in and called him, "We've gotta go now." Tru-man grabbed his connector and the shorter stack of papers and rushed out of the cave. "Angelique, Imani . . . where are they?" he asked. "They're with Pitman down below. He's guarding them . . . waiting for us," Jermaine informed him. They hid and waited, as agents passed them in the clefts, then they ran down the hill a bit. Again, they ducked and hid and waited, and when the road was clear, emerged from the rocks and ran down to meet their wives.

Halfway down the hill, they found Pitman but did not see the women. Pitman told them, "I sent the girls on ahead; they're going into the city. I told them to meet us by the tunnel I dug near where the two of you used to work. Come on, I'll show you where." Tru-man took off running, followed by Pitman and then Jermaine. "Watch out," Tru-man shouted back at them as he slowed down to duck underneath a branch protruding from the hillside. Pitman also ducked underneath it but did not warn Jermaine. Instead, upon coming up, Pitman turned back and reached for the branch. He pulled it toward himself until he felt the tension build, then, he let it go. Jermaine did not see it coming. He was hit square in the chest and face and forcefully swept from the hillside down onto the jagged rocks below. He was never heard from on this side of the great hill again. "It's just the two of us now Tru'. Just like back at Gehenna," Pitman said as he ran behind Tru-man. But Tru-man did not hear him. He was running hard to catch up to his sister and his wife. "Where's Maine?" Tru-man shouted. "I don't know. He was behind me," Pitman yelled. "But we can't stop now."

They ran through the city and finally arrived at the opening of the tunnel that Pitman had dug. Tru-man asked, "Where are the girls?" Just then, Kakei emerged from behind the side of the tree-felling company with Mr. Ruind and a unit of city agents. "The *girl* is right here," she said. Tru-man's heart skipped a beat as he began to understand the situation. He looked at Pitman and screamed, "What did you do?" Pitman stepped away from him and offered, "I can explain." But Tru-man would hear none of it. He jumped into the tunnel and began to run as hard as he could. He turned on his connector and used its light to guide him through the dark underpass, hoping to reach the great hill. His adrenalin pumping; his heart was racing and so were his thoughts—from Imani to Angelique to Jermaine—his mind was reeling from having experienced too many gains and losses in too short a time.

Just then, he thought he passed a person or, at least, a face; a very abnormal and grotesque face. But he had no time to entertain his mind's tricks; he was running for his life. That is, until he ran into a dead end. Pitman had purposely taken him to one of the unfinished tunnels. He pounded his fist against the wall that blocked him and fell to his knees. He looked down and remembered that he was still carrying the bundled pages of the book his community intended to bind. Using the light from his connector, he separated the first section which contained "The Book of Trumaine" and set it down behind a pile of dirt and rocks. Then he took one of the rocks from the pile and began carving his epitaph into the wall with large letters.

Tru-man grabbed the remaining pages of the bundle and began heading back to meet his pursuers. But he would not make it to the tunnel's entrance. Kakei and her evil ensemble met him halfway. "You should've told me you were marrying that girl. You didn't even ask if I was totally over you or care about how it would make me feel to hear about it from your bragging brother. I was going to leave you and your friends alone until I got that instant thought message from him," she explained.

Mr. Ruind looked at Kakei with a confused look as he realized that this was all touched off by a personal vendetta and not any real threat of a plot to poison the city.

Tru-man's eyes turned to Pitman. Without uttering a single word, he asked him, "How long?" Pitman began to explain, "It's not like that Tru'. When I saw how easy it was for them to find out about the wedding, I figured it would only be a matter of time before someone slipped up and gave away our location. And y'all were about to move us even further away from the city? We weren't gonna be able to stay in the hills forever man. So I figured I could work out a deal for the two of us. And it could be just like it was when we was down by Gehenna, except we wouldn't be on the run no more."

Tru-man, forcing himself to even speak to Pitman, interrogated him. "What's in it for you Pitman? What was worth selling out our whole community?" Pitman, trying to pull Tru-man into his excitement revealed, "Don't you see? They know where my wife is. They can reunite us and make things like they were before. And they have Angelique and Imani too. This deal was to save us all." But Tru-man, filled to the brim with hurt and rage, shouted, "Us all? What about Jermaine. What about the others? You're willing to trust the city?

Don't you know when people are lying to you Pitman? Or are you so blinded by your own desires?"

Just then, a voice came bellowing from halfway down the tunnel that surprised them all, "I love a man who can spot a lie the second he hears one." It was Mr. Screwtape. The moment he learned about the last-minute plan to ambush Tru-man he hid himself in the tunnel in order to uncover Kakei's real reason for wanting to raid the North Hills. "It's not a lie, is it?" Pitman asked, looking around at anyone who would respond. Screwtape walked over to put his arm around Kakei and answered him, "If I know this girl like I think I do, your wife and everyone else you just mentioned have already been violently expelled from this world. And you're soon to follow."

Screwtape turned to Tru-man and congratulated him, "Good job on the connectors. I don't know who you had helping you but no one in the media center can erase the post you sent out about your 'hilltop' experiences. Did you know it contained a virus called Preser-V that keeps replicating itself in our system?" Tru-man was not aware of the virus. But he smiled, in his heart giving credit to Angelique. Screwtape continued, "I'm not too worried about that though. We have some very creative people in our media industry who are committed to burying the books of the N.I.N.T.E.

with so much entertainment and information that people will very soon forget that your post ever appeared." Screwtape looked hard but was concerned when he saw that Tru-man seemed unmoved by his plans to intentionally distract people from reading the N.I.N.T.E.'s digital book.

"Do you think that the two physical copies you made will be enough to carry on your legacy?" Screwtape rhetorically asked in frustration. "We found the one copy you left in the North Hills and the one you're holding in your hands is about to be destroyed." A city agent stepped forward and wrestled the bundle away from Tru-man. "I mean really, two copies?" Mr. Ruind said as he laughed a condescending laugh. Screwtape plucked a cigar from the inner pocket of his coat, the long coat he always wore and never removed. Then he lit his cigar. Watching Tru-man carefully, he used his cigar to light the bundle of papers on fire. Tru-man looked at the burning pages and wondered if the combination of flames, pages written about Newman by his friends and the presence of Newman's enemies would be enough to summon him to come to the rescue like he did back at Gehenna.

Screwtape turned to Pitman and told him, "Kill the Free-hand and this might work out for you." He ordered this mainly to hurt Kakei for lying to him in the first place. Kakei's eyes widened. She never had any intentions of seeing Tru-man killed. She only wanted to destroy his marriage to Angelique. But she knew that she could not protest a single word spoken by Mr. Screwtape. Her only hope was Pitman, who could not even look at Tru-man, let alone advance upon him. Then Mr. Ruind threatened Pitman saying, "Kill him Ace, or we'll kill you." Ruind called him Ace because, all night long, Kakei kept referring to Pitman as her ace after he unexpectedly contacted her and offered to give up information about Tru-man's last minute wedding change and the N.I.N.T.E.'s location in exchange for his wife's release. After a momentary pause, Pitman firmly gripped the pickaxe left sticking out of the wall by his work crew and swung it wildly until it came to rest in Tru-man's shoulder, who tried to block the blow. Tru-man, hurt just as much by the betrayal as the axe, fell against the wall of the tunnel.

Pitman turned to his new associates to see whether he had done enough to prove his allegiance to them. But Screwtape, who had betrayed countless people over the course of his long existence, commanded Mr. Ruind to, "Kill him too," for he passionately and hypocritically hated traitors with the entirety of his heartless soul. Then, Ruind instructed his agents, who were thugs at heart, to do what they would to Pitman. The agents began grabbing nearby rocks that had been picked loose and, one by one, caused the weight of their stones to end Pitman's life. Tru-man watched and pitied him while Mr. Ruind laughed. "What's so funny?" Kakei asked, disgusted by the way things were turning out. He explained his inside joke, "You said you always keep an ace in the hole. And his name is Pitman. Looks like no matter what we call this guy, he was destined to end up in the ground." He laughed some more and then motioned for the agents to do the same to Tru-man.

They began to attack the wounded Tru-man, but would not throw their stones with the same force they had used against Pitman, for as they looked upon the angelic innocence of his face, they were each filled with shame. Then Tru-man turned towards the great hill and the ground above him began to quake open. He was sure that he could see, even from the great distance, Newman standing beside his father waiting to receive him again as a guest on his hill. Everyone else ran out of the tunnel and left him there to die. And he did.

Upon returning to the surface, Mr. Screwtape was sure that Tru-man was hiding something. But he could not imagine what it might be. So, being the cunning individual that he was, he quickly devised an insurance plan to counter whatever Tru-man was up to. He commanded Mr. Ruind, "Send your men back down to get the body of Trumaine. We need to send a message to his followers and anybody in the city that might be fooled by the N.I.N.T.E.'s post. And tell your agents not to do anything to the documents they found in the North Hills. Bring me every page of that book." Ruind got on his connector and sent the word to preserve the manuscripts. Then he asked Screwtape why he now wanted to save the fugitives' writings. Screwtape responded, "We must always stay a step ahead of our enemies. And I have a feeling that having their documents in our possession might come in handy in the future." And it did.

Episode FIVE

Shadowless City

It was a cool summer day when Khalil went to the play grounds to hang out with his friends. There was no sign posted, but everyone at the play grounds seemed to understand the unwritten rules: children under ten play in the colorful section; teens play in the sports section; and adults can check on either of the two but are mostly only welcomed over by the benches. As he reached the sports area, one of his friends called to him, "Lil'man are you lost? Shouldn't you be over there in the colorful section?" Khalil laughed it off. He used to like his nickname but, as his friends outgrew him in height, the name began to bother him more and more.

Lil'man, or Khalil Freeman as he was named at birth, turned to sports as a way to win back the respect his lack of height seemed to be costing him. He bested his friends in almost every aspect of the games they played: running, jumping, catching, and throwing; but all this only made them jealous and look for more ways to cast shade upon his shining moments. There was another reason for his friends' jealousy, but like his height, it was something that he thought would never change.

After a good game, the group of friends went to rest their tired, youthful frames up against the fence that separated the sports section from the colorful section. Khalil usually hated standing beside his friends on that fence, even when he needed the rest, but today he did not mind. He knew that there would not be as much teasing as usual because it was a cool day and the sun was not making fun of him by casting long shadows on the ground of everyone except him. As they stood there, Khalil listened to the children in the next section play the games he used to play when he was a child. The most popular game was called "90 and the City." The 90 team was pure evil and the City team was the good guys. One lucky youngster got to wear the long coat and play

Mr. Screwtape. And some unlucky child on the 90 team was forced to be Newman, who of course, always had to lose in the play grounds because, as they were taught, Newman lost in real life.

By the time Khalil turned five and began playing in the colorful section, the story of how Mr. Screwtape fought off the big bad band of the 90 was already legendary and being taught to children. But now he was turning 16 in a couple of weeks (his birthday was on the same day as his father's) and if he so desired, he could become a junior city agent. However, Khalil was different from other young boys. He did not cherish the idea of becoming a city agent like his friends. Most teens were taught by their parents that the 90 no longer existed and that only children still pretend to be fighting against Newman. Still, in their hearts, the young men of Nameless City hoped that they could one day be like Mr. Screwtape and defeat the threat of terror from the hills; be it Newman, the 90 or any of Newman's other friends that might be hiding there. The hills were for the enemies of the city and it had been that way for the last forty-two years, ever since the deaths of Tru-man and Jermaine.

Mr. Taskman and Mr. Ruind had passed away some years ago. Mr. Conman was now an aged man at sixty-four years old, still running the media center and teaching young people to follow in his steps. Kakei, who was only two years younger than Mr. Conman, had married Mr. Screwtape and undergone numerous cosmetic surgeries in order to keep herself looking young and attractive for him. But he had long since stopped paying attention to her. He enjoyed seeing her battle with self-esteem issues while shivering from the chills of his cold shoulder. She stayed with him because she had become possessed with the idea of visiting the underground mall as he strung her along with promises to eventually take her. As for Mr. Screwtape, he looked to be about fifty-five years old, but had the kind of face that one would not be surprised to learn that he was twenty years older or younger than he appeared. But no one knew his true age.

Mr. Screwtape had been working on a plan to increase the number of Halfway's-house fast food restaurants in the city. This plan promised homeowners that if they gave up their homes for him to build on their land, they would receive living space in the new condos being built behind the great hill, as well as, huge discounts on everything in the underground mall once it was restored to its original state. Screwtape had still not become the Supreme Head of Nameless City but was getting closer to his goal. He was working on his original treaty and the housing plan with the new city controller Ivan Ben

Ruind the 3rd, the grandson of Mr. Ruind. Until the condos were ready, individuals who gave up their homes were forced to move in with family members or live in group homes with other people who had taken the Screwtape deal. But the homes were becoming increasingly crowded.

On this cool summer day, Ruind the 3rd, or Iv'Ben, as he was commonly called, brought up this over-crowded housing issue in a meeting with Mr. Screwtape. "How much longer do we have on the condo and mall project? My people are getting tired of living in these group homes." Screwtape assured him that it would not be much longer but that he should stress patience to his people. If there was one thing Mr. Screwtape had, it was patience. He had learned to wait years and years before a plan of his was actually put in motion and fully carried out.

But Iv'Ben had more concerns. He continued, "What about the men who've gone up the great hill to build for you? Why haven't they come back? And why can't I go up to see the progress on the condos or the mall?" Screwtape turned to Mr. Conman who sat quietly in the meeting. Conman smiled and shook his head as if to say, "It's not the boy's fault. He's just too young to understand." Screwtape told Iv'Ben, "I'll talk to my boss and see what's happening with the workers. And I'll see about getting you a permit to go to the building site." "You have a boss?" Iv'Ben asked, his voice full of surprise. "I was told that there was no one over you." But Screwtape informed him, "There will be no one over me in Nameless City once our deal goes through, but I'm only an ambassador to this place. Now, is that all? I have some other important business to attend to."

Iv'Ben pulled out his connector and opened up an air chart which projected from his screen and created a hologram-graph in mid-air. "There's one more thing," he said. "Our scientists tell me that we're in for a very cold winter this year; much, much colder than normal as you can see from this chart. I've been told that years ago there was a tree-felling company here in the city and that the trees had all been cut down to prepare for such a time as this, so I'd like to know where all those trees are being stored so that we can be ready for the cold." Mr. Conman smiled, knowing that the young city controller was in for a surprise. "I'll check on it and get back to you," Screwtape said, pretending for the moment that he did not mind answering to the young official. Then he escorted Iv'Ben to the door.

"Do you really have a boss?" Conman asked Screwtape. To which, he nodded his head, "Yes." "When are you gonna tell young Iv'Ben about the trees?" Conman asked. "I haven't decided yet?"

Screwtape replied in a confused tone. "I thought we made up that nonsense about the city getting colder in order to convince his grandfather to cut down the trees. But those charts . . . ," Screwtape thought out loud. "Yeah, that was kind of creepy. Maybe it's just a weird coincidence," Conman offered. "Maybe," said Screwtape, "But we've gotta start getting people up the great hill into the condos or there's gonna be a problem." "Agreed," Conman said, right before he made a personal request for his aging self.

"Screwtape, let me ask you something. Once we start moving people halfway up the great hill into those condos, there won't be as much use for an old man like myself down in the city. I've got young people at the media center who know all my tricks . . . well, almost all of my tricks," he laughed. "Do you think you could save me a spot up there beyond the great hill?" But Screwtape, who was lying about the condos in the first place, hated even the idea of giving anything to anyone who hadn't very recently done something for him. So he responded, "You know Conman, you've been very useful. Your schemes have helped my schemes very well over the years. So, if you can prove yourself more useful to me now than you've been in the past, I will make sure that you have a place halfway up the hill." Mr. Conman had learned that this was the best he could expect from Mr. Screwtape. The old friends shook on it and then parted company until their next meeting.

Another week had gone by and Khalil was back in the play grounds locked in a heated debate with his friends about conspiracy theories. It all started after Khalil had missed and messed up several plays during a game against another group of boys. The whole game, he was busy looking at the ground, fascinated by the fact that the sun was shining as bright as ever and yet no one appeared to have a shadow. As they stood by the fence, he brought it up again asking, "When's the last time y'all remember making a joke about me being so short that I don't even have a shadow?" Rodman, the oldest and tallest of the bunch, who always cast the longest shadow and made the first joke about it, stopped and thought. He moved around until he finally found an angle where his shadow could be somewhat seen. "Look," Rodmad shouted excitedly, "here's my shadow." Khalil pointed out the fact that it was mid-summer and yet the weather had been consistently cool, feeling like the middle of fall. He was convinced that something strange was happening.

One of his friends responded, "Man, I don't know how the grandson of Mr. Screwtape and Lady Kakei could be such a 90-lover." But one of the others, named Dayman, corrected him, "That's because he's not the grandson of Mr. Screwtape. Lady Kakei already had a son before Mr. Screwtape found her and married her. That's where Lil'man comes from." Khalil's connection to the city's leaders was the real reason behind his friends' envy. But the twisted rumors surrounding his grandmother's premarital pregnancy by another man was also the reason Khalil hated his last name even more than his nickname. He always wondered how much better his life would be if he had been born a Screwtape instead of Freeman, especially since he never knew his real grandfather.

Khalil corrected Dayman, "I'm not a 90-lover. The stuff I talk about is not in favor of the 90 or Newman. I just question whether or not the city has our best interest in heart when they introduce new programs." He had learned to distrust the city from his father, who had learned this distrust from Khalil's grandmother, Kakei. Just as much as he wanted to prove to his friends that he was not a 90-lover, he confused them by always being equally suspicious of the city's agenda.

Dayman attempted to sum up Khalil's position, "You want us to believe that the city cut down all the trees years ago, and then waited until everyone forgot; and is now causing us to have a cold summer just so they can sell us firewood?" "Or something like that," Khalil responded. But Dayman was quick with his rebuttal, "I haven't seen one commercial for firewood pop up on my connector, have any of you?" "Nope," they all answered. Dayman continued, "And, how would they have control over the weather, or whether or not we see our shadows? I mean, I know you're related to them and all but, how powerful do you think these people are?" The group laughed. Then Rodman added, "That's just like the time you were trying to tell us that the media center hires entertainers to trick us into going into Gehenna, and that the famous people don't get their flashy chains from going through the great fire into the underground mall. How did you say they get all that stuff again?" The group laughed and Khalil felt even more ashamed for having bought into his father's suspicion. But he had no reason to be ashamed because his father was right.

Years ago, right after the death of Tru-man, Mr. Conman was commissioned by Screwtape to come up with a way to use the media to distract people from paying attention to the sixty-six books of the N.I.N.T.E. Conman knew that people liked to see fantastic and unbelievable things when they tuned in to the media so he created an entire industry based on showing the wildest things imaginable. Mr. Screwtape gave him the idea to build up a fantasy about an entrance to the underground mall located somewhere behind the fires of Gehenna. To do this, Conman used male and female entertainers who sang and rapped about doing the impossible—going through the great fire which burns continually and coming back with merchandise from the underground mall. These entertainers did not really do this, of course. But the public did not know that. People marveled and wondered how their favorite entertainers were getting all of their new flashy things.

In reality, Screwtape had worked out a deal with his boss, the owner of that false food restaurant halfway up the hill. The deal was that Screwtape would send entertainers up the hill to the SOUL FOOLED restaurant after they bragged about going into Gehenna. Once there, the owner of that place would give them extended time in the cash and carry room which contained stolen items from the underground mall. Then, the owner would allow some of them to come back down the hill without being attacked by Curse and Consequence. In exchange, Screwtape told the owner, many people down in the city will think that the way to get those flashy things is to enter into the great fire. And when regular people begin to go into Gehenna to be like these celebrities, they can be snatched up and imprisoned in the underground mall.

Conman knew nothing of this secret deal between Screwtape and his boss. He knew that Screwtape was from the Chain Linked Nation, so he assumed that the flashy chains and new merchandise was just something Screwtape could afford to give away. All Conman wanted was for people to buy his media content which made the impossible look possible. He did not take into consideration how many people would try to imitate the artists. Screwtape, on the other hand, enjoyed seeing people get burned or consumed by Gehenna and imprisoned in the underground mall as they tried to live the life that the entertainers portrayed. Even some of the entertainers themselves began to be fooled by other entertainers who told fascinating stories about going through Gehenna and not getting burned.

As Khalil and his friends debated these conspiracy theories, Dayman decided to settle at least one of them. He proposed, "Alright, then let's test it. For the next two weeks let's go down and camp out by Gehenna every night and see if we spot any entertainers going into the great fire and coming back with merchandise from the underground mall." They all thought that it would be fun and exciting, so they agreed to take on the mission.

It was not difficult for the boys to get their parents' permission. All of them were of the age where they should be looking to become junior city agents, and so, their parents encouraged them in the adventure. Khalil's father was not so much interested in his son preparing to serve the city; he simply liked the fact that Khalil was questioning what the media was saying and showing to him. His only concern came in the form of, "I know it's summertime, but it's been cold so just make sure you take enough blankets to keep warm down there." "Dad, it's Gehenna. I don't think there's a warmer place in the whole world," he replied. And with that, Khalil was off to meet his friends.

As they traveled south through the woods, Khalil laughed and mentioned that he was not the only one who seemed to be dressed more for nighttime in the fall than a summer evening. The other teens remarked that the weather did seem a bit strange but that it was not as severe as what Khalil was suggesting. They finally reached the end of the woods and began to build their campsites about fifty yards from one another. They each would use their connectors to alert the others if indeed they happened to spot someone going into or coming out of the fires. The first two nights no one showed up and nothing happened. On the third night however, Rodman called the group over to his camp.

When they all arrived, he informed them that a new singer who had recently become very popular was attempting to go into the flames. They all watched with awe as the entertainer readied himself for the feat. Then, they heard the faint counting of "one, two, three!" On "three," the singer lunged forward into Gehenna's flashing lights. Once in the fire, he jumped around in pain and after about five seconds, it began to look as if the fire, or something in the fire, was trying to grab hold of him. The singer leaped out of the burning trash heap and rolled around on the ground until his blazing body was extinguished.

The teens ran down to help him and after making sure he was okay, they asked, "Does it usually work for you?" But he did not answer them. Then Khalil said, "In your songs you say 'it's nothing'; that you do it all the time with no consequences. Is this your first time getting burned?" But the singer said, "Tell me your names. I'll make sure you get paid and receive gifts from the underground mall if you never tell anyone what you saw here tonight." Some of the young men gave their names but others were too disappointed to do so.

When he left, Khalil asked his friends, "Do we need to stay here another night? Haven't we seen enough?" But Dayman answered, "I never said that some of them don't get burned by doing the stuff they sing about. But this is about the ones who actually do make it through and come back with stuff. We're still waiting to see that." And so they went back to their campsites. It was late. After the boys talked for a while through their connectors about their experience, they fell asleep.

Meanwhile, Mr. Screwtape was meeting with his boss. "Are any of those city workers still alive," he asked. "I need you to send some of them back down the hill; preferably the ones you haven't treated too badly yet. People are asking questions and I can use them to buy more time." The owner agreed; he had several city workers whom he was still toying with and hadn't fed to the lions or put into captivity in the underground mall. "You know I don't like going into those stores," the owner of SOUL FOOD said. "I don't want to spend one second longer than I have to in there. But I'll have someone go in and bring out the men who haven't realized that they're suffering yet." Screwtape began to head toward the exit but turned back to ask, "Oh yeah, do you know anything about why the city is getting colder? I told a lie about the city freezing years ago and now it seems to be coming true."

"No," the owner snapped back nastily. He had many evil schemes going but he hated being blamed for ones that he had no part in. "I don't care about the temperature of that cursed city. Whatever is happening there is your problem. But use your head for once you useless idiot. If it's getting colder, that's all the more reason to encourage those fools to move toward Gehenna. And once they do, find a way to push them in. I'm not going to live caged up in that damned abandoned mall forever without them." Feeling belittled and embarrassed, Screwtape put back on his long coat and left through the loading dock at the back of the underground mall. Then, he mentally prepared himself to do what he hated doing most—entering the Nameless City through the fires of Gehenna.

As Khalil lay asleep at his campsite, he heard a scream that sounded as if someone was being tortured. He awoke and, before he could clear his eyes to focus, thought he saw in the distance a face lit with flames. At least, it had the appearance of a face, but a very grotesque and abnormal one. As he shook off the sleep, he saw a man walking away from the fire in a long overcoat. He recognized the figure as his grandmother's husband so he did not alert his friends. He ran to meet him and asked whether anyone had entered Gehenna. Mr. Screwtape asked him what he was doing in the woods and when Khalil told him, Screwtape laughed. "Don't believe the stuff you see in the media, Khalil. No one gets all that flashy stuff you see by going into

Gehenna. You'd have to be something out of this world to walk through those flames and not get burned. You understand?"

Khalil shook his head in affirmation. Then Screwtape told him, "One day I'll work it out so that you can go halfway up the hill and, maybe, just maybe you might come back with some bling." Screwtape cared enough to keep Khalil from the fires, but not enough to keep him from his boss. He kept walking but looked back to tell his wife's grandson, "Oh, about that whole 'not believing what you see in the media' . . . do me a favor, don't tell your friends. I'm sure Mr. Conman would appreciate it if we let them believe in his magic for a little while longer." Khalil shook his head in agreement. The next day, he went home and did not go back down to Gehenna with his friends.

The next day, down at the city center, Ivan Ben Ruind the 3rd had a private meeting with the city's scientists and meteorologists to determine what was happening to the weather. "We have some startling data to report," the chief scientist said. "When the city cut down the trees over forty years ago, the available oxygen in our atmosphere was diminished but, for the most part, we naturally adjusted and learned to live off the oxygen produced by the plant life in the woods and the hills surrounding us." "Go on," Iv'Ben said. "Well sir," the scientist continued, "Without trees to trap the carbon dioxide we produce, those gasses are left to linger in our atmosphere which should have made things warmer. Also, if the trees were burned, they would have released carbon dioxide into the atmosphere; this also would have made things warmer. But it doesn't seem like that happened.

"We thought that maybe, if they burned even a small number of the trees, that an ash cloud was produced that has somehow risen into the stratosphere and is now blocking the sun from making full contact with our city's surface." "And?" Iv'Ben asked. The man continued, "Well, when we went to measure the amount of radiation coming from the sun, we found that . . ." But the scientist had a hard time with what he was about to say. "Spit it out!" Iv'Ben demanded. "It appears that the sun is moving further away from us," he said. Iv'Ben could not believe what he had just heard. "What do mean 'it appears'?" he asked. "Well," the man continued, "It only appears that way sometimes. We can't tell if it's the sun moving, or if it's us moving further from the sun. Everything in space seems to be spreading apart." "Well move us back closer!" Ivan Ben Ruind the 3rd demanded irrationally.

The chief scientist ignored the absurd comment from the city controller and then informed him that the temperature would continue to drop and that, at some point, life would be unsustainable on the planet's surface. They estimated five years if the planet and the sun continued moving away from one another at the current rate. But, they informed him, the distancing speed was not constant; rather, it was constantly changing.

Iv'Ben ran from the meeting and upstairs to the office of Mr. Screwtape. He reported the news and panicked. But Screwtape knew there was only one person powerful enough to have caused such a cataclysmic shift in cosmic events, and this power rested double the distance of his boss' residence only halfway up the hill. Knowing that his time was limited, Screwtape needed to get as many people into Gehenna as possible if he was to accomplish his mission. Iv'Ben asked him, "How many trees do we have stored away, maybe we can begin burning them to create more greenhouse gasses and warm things back up." Screwtape told him, "There are no trees. Your grandfather burned them all." He then told the young city controller, "Put out a public message from the city warning everyone that we are moving into a state of emergency. Say enough to satisfy the scientists but not enough to cause a widespread panic.

"Tell everyone that they are to move towards Gehenna within the next two months. We will be closing the Halfway's-houses in the city and building new ones in the woods to encourage people to move. Tell them the city is getting colder and it will be that way for quite a while, but things will be back to normal soon. Tell them the condos behind the great hill will be finished soon, and the mall is almost done. We will be moving into them by the end of the year; the people in the group homes first, and then others on the waiting list. But listen, we can't fit everyone in the condos and the mall. We need to complete our treaty. If I become Supreme Head of Nameless City, I will be in a better position to negotiate a deal with my boss to bring the rest of your people into my realm. Do what you have to do to move up the vote on this issue.

"Tell your citizens that we will all be gathering down by the fires to keep warm and get ourselves organized into groups, so the closer they are to Gehenna, the better." Iv'Ben shook his head and turned to go put the plan into action but Mr. Screwtape called him back to warn him, "Don't try to answer too many questions about the mall, Gehenna or the trees. If you do, they'll blame your grandfather and then you. And they'll be right. So get them focused on the future, not the past." Screwtape said this to keep the focus off of himself, but his young mentee fell for his trickery.

The news went out from connector to connector. But no one really knew what to think. If they had two months to move, was it really an emergency. However, the partial news about the city getting colder made sense. Everyone felt it and noticed the early winter conditions at the height of summer. Khalil got the message and went to go visit his father at work, where the tree-felling company used to be. He couldn't wait to brag about the fact that he noticed the atmospheric change long before anyone in the media announced it. On every street he passed, people were talking to one another about how strange things were getting in the city.

Just then, the ground began to quake and the whole city shook violently. A woman, who had just come out of the building across from where his father worked, suddenly disappeared. She had fallen beneath the surface through a giant crack in the sidewalk. When the ground stopped shaking, Khalil and a few others ran to help her out of the hole. She made it up safely but then realized that her pocketbook was still under the ground. Everyone looked around until all eyes landed on Khalil. "You're small enough lil' buddy, why don't you hop down there and get it," one of them said. Once again, despising his height, Khalil allowed himself to be lowered down into the whole. "Use your connector as a light," the woman shouted. He pulled out his device and aimed it at the ground, but he noticed right away how hollow the space seemed to be; too hollow to have been caused by the earthquake.

"Do you see it?" the woman shouted. He had already forgotten to look for her purse. "Still looking," he shouted back as he turned his light toward the ground again. As he scanned the surface, he spotted the stacked bundle of pages that Tru-man had tucked behind the pile of rocks four decades ago. This intrigued him. He quickly turned to locate the woman's pocketbook and upon finding it, he scooped it up and tossed it out through the opening. "Alright lil' man, now you. C'mon," a man called to him, reaching down to pull him up. But Khalil felt that he was meant to find those pages in that tunnel that day. He called back, "Nah, that's alright. I can get up on my own. Y'all can go ahead." "The ground may not be done quaking. If it starts again, you'll be crushed," said the voice from above. But he would not leave. He moved to the back of the tunnel and reached down to recover the dirt showered manuscript. The youngster then sat down and crossed his legs and began to read "The Book of Trumaine."

He read about Tru-man's journey up the great hill, how Newman rescued him, his experience at Newman's restaurant at the top of the hill and how the owner of the SOUL FOOLED restaurant aimed to disrupt Newman's plan for the city. Then he read the part that struck him most—Newman's account of how Uman and his wife disregarded Newman and his father.

One day, my father sent an invitation for Uman and his wife Evelyn to meet us for lunch, but none of my employees could find them. So I went looking for them just as the day began to cool, only to find that they had gone to that false food restaurant halfway up the hill. They had been inside for days, trapped by Curse and Consequence but, also, by their guilt. They were hiding out in that wicked establishment, hoping to not have to come out and answer to me. I stood on the path and shouted for them to come to the door, but they told themselves that I was only shouting because I found them at that wicked restaurant. Then, Uman came to the door and blamed Evelyn for leading him into SOUL FOOLED. Evelyn came to the door and told me how the owner had tricked her and that now, they cannot leave and must live with Curse and Consequence.

After talking for a while, Uman wanted to make a run for the path that led back to me, believing that the beasts could not reach him. But Evelyn was terrified of the lions. I cautioned Uman about the danger of coming toward me, while at the same time I comforted Evelyn that everything would work out and be okay. Then, I did what I had planned to do. In order for Uman and Evelyn to escape Curse and Consequence, I knew that someone would have to distract the beasts. But the only thing that would distract them was another body for them to gnaw on in place Uman and Evelyn's. I would have instantly sacrificed myself to save them but I knew that Curse and Consequence would not attack me the way I was. And so, I left.

For plotting against me and Uman, I closed down the underground mall and locked most of those evil ex-employees of mine inside of the stores. Those ex-employees who were not trapped were left to roam back and forth through the corridors of the mall. I placed a great fire outside of the mall's back entrance so that those wicked workers could not easily pass into the city. Then I remained up at the top of the hill for forty-two years. Time moved slower back then. Those forty-

two years felt more like forty-two generations. Uman and Evelyn lived a long time, as most people did back then. They started a family and had a lot of children, who went on to have a lot of children. They all lived in that limited space between the SOUL FOOLED restaurant and the other end of the mall.

The owner of that poisonous place, who controls nothing but the lion's chains, was allowed to shackle all of Uman's children with chains binding their hands to their neck. I allowed this for two reasons: one, to remind them of the lions awaiting them; and two, to limit their ability to do damage to themselves and others after eating the false food served in that place. I told the owner to use two chains: a heavy one to remind them of Curse, and another lighter chain, no longer than 120 links, to remind them of Consequence. But I didn't just leave it up to him. I made sure that all of Uman's children were branded with an image of those two beasts, one on each hand. The images can only be seen on the hill, or by my employees and ex-employees. There was only one rule: if anyone was ever born without those images, the owner would not be allowed to chain that person.

As Uman's children grew, they tried to break into the stores to retrieve the goods that were still there. Often, they were enticed by my wicked ex-employees. But instead of bringing anything out of the stores, they found themselves trapped behind the gates they tried to crash, unable to enjoy the things that tempted them in the first place. At some point, almost all of Uman's children tried to exit through the front, but everyone who did was consumed by those insatiable lions.

Finally, after those long years, I returned. Not through the front door, but through a secret entrance to the mall that only I knew about. I disguised myself to look more like Uman, or one of his children, so that I could live there among them. I wanted to experience what life had been like for them trapped in that gloomy place. My ex-employees recognized me almost immediately, but I was there for many years without Uman and Evelyn even realizing who I was. It broke my heart to see how Uman developed an appetite for the false-food served in that place. And even more to see that he had passed that appetite on to his children. They were born with a natural hunger for that harmful food. I spent all my time making meals to feed people and showing them how content their souls were meant to be. I made a lot of friends, but a lot of enemies too. I spoke so much about my father's restaurant at the top of the hill that, after a while, my skeptics and enemies began daring me to leave the SOUL FOOD restaurant to prove that I had come from, or could actually get back to the top of the hill, or that I could at least make it past Curse and Consequence.

It wasn't long before they began setting me up to have me thrown out of SOUL FOOLED. They wanted to discredit me by showing that Curse and Consequence could treat me the same as anyone else. But they didn't know that I had always planned to leave through those doors. I wasn't looking forward to being attacked by the deadly duo, but I was looking forward to making a way for Uman and Evelyn to come back to my father. And so, eventually, I let my enemies' plot against me succeed.

When the day finally came for me to take my exit from that place, they made me walk from one end of the mall to the other. The whole time, they were taking votes from each person I passed asking, "Should we throw this man out?" Then someone started a chant which the whole crowd took up and joined in, "To the lions; to the lions." I even heard some of my friends voices among the crowd. When my enemies saw that the crowd approved of my death, they began to abuse me. I cannot tell you all the things they did to injure me; it would hurt you to hear it. I got closer to the doors of that deadly diner. On the other side, I could see Curse and Consequence watching me carefully as they began preparing for their meal.

But, also, waiting inside by the door was Uman and Evelyn. They did not spend much time in the mall but always stood by the doors, looking to road, waiting for me to return as I told them I would many years before. They did not know that I had been there with them for over thirty years. They turned their aged faces and strained their tired eyes until they realized who I was, and once they did, the excitement filled them to overflowing. I cautioned them not to use my real name. "Call me Newman," I said. That was the new name my father gave me for the mission. And they did as they leapt for joy. "We've been hearing about 'Newman' for years, but had no idea that YOU were Him," they said with gladness. "Get ready to run back to my father," I told them. Then, before my enemies could say or do another thing to me, I ran through the doors and gave myself to the lions, wrestling with them while shouting for Uman and Evelyn to run back to the road.

The beasts clawed and chewed at me all they could and at one point, they were quite sure that they had killed me as my lifeless body bounced back and forth between them. But they were only used to attacking people with chained hands, whereas I was fully free and able to attack them back. We wrestled and fought for over three hours but, I'm sure to those lions, it felt more like three days. After I conquered them, they finally realized who I was. The whole time, the owner of that soul ruining restaurant just stood at the door and watched in awe. When I finally got back to the road, I saw that instead of running towards the top of the hill, most of Uman's children had run out of SOUL FOOLED and headed down into the city, just as I thought they might. The owner of SOUL FOOLED had filled their heads and hearts with so many lies about my father and I, so that no matter how much I called for them to come up the hill, they only ran harder and farther to get away from me.

But they were unaware that I don't just own the restaurant at the top of the hill. I own the hill. And I own the city. I had even named it, but I removed my name from the city and let them inhabit it so that they could see what life down there would be like without me. They built their homes according to the design of the owner of the SOUL FOOLED establishment. In fact, he used Uman's children to build his Halfway's-house restaurants all over the city and even now, they continue to rely on him for their food— dying a slow death-by-diet. But from time to time, my father draws men and women to his hill. He sends the breeze which carries the aroma of our appetizers down into the city and those who sense it cannot help but to travel up the hill to, perhaps, be found by that which they hope to find.

But, as I'm sure you already know, not everyone senses the scent. Some go further and further away from the great hill and end up in another place. Gehenna's fire was not originally for Uman and Evelyn, or their children, but it does serve a purpose concerning them. I knew that Uman's children would be tempted to try to enter the mall from the south, but I did not want them going in there until I had dealt with our common enemy. And even though many have tried to enter, those fires now serve to warn men and women not to go after the things I have in store for them without coming all the way up the hill to go through me.

The light from Khalil's connector began to flicker and then went out. Like everything else in Nameless City, the device was solar powered but the retreating sun had stopped forcing its rays down into the gloomy tunnel where he sat. All that time, Khalil had not moved an inch except to turn the pages of Truman's book. He considered what it would all mean if the things he read were actually true. But how could they be? All his life, he had been taught that Newman was a threat, and that his Grandmother's husband, Mr. Screwtape, had saved the city from him. In his heart, Khalil spoke a bold thing to Newman, "If this book is telling the truth about you, you need to give me a sign . . . just one." He waited for a moment, but nothing happened. However, when he tried to stand up his legs locked from sitting so long in the same position. As he fell backwards to the ground, his connector's light turned back on and lit up the entire wall. Khalil could not believe what he saw there. Or could he?

There on the wall was the inscription left by Tru-man, just as fresh as the day he carved it. In giant letters it read N I N T E. But the letters were spread far apart. As Khalil looked closer, he saw smaller letters in between the large ones which helped to spell out what he needed to know— NEWMAN IS NOT THE ENEMY. Khalil quickly spidered backwards, away from the wall, fearing that the message had been written just then when he spoke to Newman in his heart. He grabbed the pages of Tru-man's book and climbed up through the opening in the surface above. Then he ran to the one person he thought would be able to give him the truth—his grandmother.

Upon arriving, he was welcomed, hugged and kissed in the grandmotherly fashion. She offered him some fast food, which he normally would not turn down. Having fast food in the home was one of the few perks that came along with being married to Mr. Screwtape. "No," he said, still catching his breath.

Khalil had decided that he would try his best to go without the Halfway's fast food until he got some answers. "I've gotta talk to you Grandma' K." They walked further in and sat down. Just as he began to reveal his discovery, Mr. Screwtape walked in. "Is this a private meeting?" he asked jokingly. "No," Khalil answered, "Maybe you can help too." "Okay, what's going on Lil'man?" Screwtape said as he sat down. Khalil had to fight the urge to tell him how much he now hated being called Lil'man. It was Screwtape who gave him the nickname and it was well known how bad he took it whenever someone rejected him or anything that he had given. Looking away and swallowing his pride, Khalil focused on a nearby picture of Mr. Screwtape and Kakei, taken when they were younger; or at least, when Kakei was younger, since Mr. Screwtape looked pretty much the same.

Khalil began, "Okay, have either of you ever heard of a guy named Trumaine?" Kakei dropped the tray of food she was holding but Screwtape squeezed her hard in order to steady her. "No, we haven't," Screwtape said for her. "Who's he?" Khalil pulled out the recently unburied treasure. "I found this. It looks like it was supposed to go into a book. Mr. Screwtape, I've heard all the stories about how you defeated the 90; but is that the same as the N.I.N.T.E.?" he spelled out the letters. "According to this, we've had it all wrong. There is supposedly this restaurant in the hills somewhere. It doesn't say which hill, but based on the way it's written, I think it's the hill behind the food court at the end of Straight Street. And the N.I.N.T.E. is not a number; it's an acrostic that stands for Newman Is Not The Enemy. I think someone is trying to tell me, or us, something. Mr. Screwtape, you fought the 90, but I never heard any stories about you actually fighting Newman. Maybe there's more to the story that we don't know about. What do you guys think?" As Khalil went on about the book, Screwtape smiled, realizing now that he had been tricked by Tru-man into thinking he burned the entire copy of the N.I.N.T.E.'s book.

But Screwtape was prepared. He told the youngster, "Well, have you ever smelled an aroma coming down from the hill? All I ever smell is the aroma of sweet fast food. But if you think there's something to it, maybe we should search for more documents and see if there really is a book of the N.I.N.T.E. out there." Kakei could not believe her ears. She smiled and said, "Yeah, maybe. I trust the city will make the right decision." Khalil thought that was a strange response coming from the woman who had taught his father not to trust the city. Screwtape got up quickly and excused himself from the room while Kakei smiled a nervous smile. Khalil also excused himself and rushed out to show his friends the proof that his conspiracy theories were more than just theories.

The next morning he arranged to meet with his friends in the play grounds where he put on an exhibit for all who were within an earshot. As he spoke, the adults came from the benches and the children from the colorful section. They stood around him, rubbing their hands and arms to keep warm. The scene was an odd one. It was 10:30 in the morning and yet it looked to be about six or seven in the evening. The sun was high in the sky but it didn't seem to matter.

As Khalil spoke, some began to heckle and mock him until, he scanned the pages of Tru-man's book with his connector and displayed the results to the crowd. The laughter stopped when they saw that the pages had indeed been written forty-two years ago and had been buried beneath the city since then. People began video recording Khalil with their connectors and sending the clips to their friends. Meanwhile, Mr. Screwtape told Mr. Conman to change the media's security encryption so that people could once again send and receive messages containing Newman's name. But Screwtape had also put another part of his plan into action.

While Khalil was speaking, someone shouted, "The kid must be right. I just got an alert on my connector saying 'Forty-year-old documents found.'" Someone else confirmed, "Yeah, I just got one that says, 'Message from the past, were we wrong about Newman?'" Khalil was excited to think that his Grandmother's husband had believed him and acted so swiftly on his discovery. But then, someone in the crowd shouted, "This kid is screwing around with us. It says here that there were over 130 old books found bound together. It says the first one is called "The Book of Trumaine" but the other books make the message in that book much clearer. They have hired an expert named Mr. Shaman to interpret the meaning of the writings."

Someone else added, "Listen to this. I just got a message that says a kid, around 16 years old, found the books in a cave in the North Hills after the earthquake and turned them over to the city. But it says that another kid who was with him ripped out the first book and ran off with it. They can't find him and without that first book, they can't interpret the rest." Everyone in the crowd paused and looked around, then turned back to look at Khalil. Khalil looked at Rodman who shouted, "Run!"

Khalil took off running from the play grounds. Rodman held back as many people as he could while

Dayman and the rest of the teens helped with the escape. They crisscrossed one another in and out of traffic, passing the rolled up pages back and forth to confuse their pursuers. Khalil, who had not eaten fast food since he found Tru-man's book, was running slower than usual. Rodman caught up with him and received the scroll and then broke away down an alley between two buildings. Their plan was to meet back up at one of their old hangout spots on the other side of the city.

After about thirty minutes, Khalil made it to the rendezvous. Then Dayman showed up; and then a few others. They turned off their connectors, afraid that city agents were now searching for them in light of the recent reports about the stolen pages. An hour had gone by and Rodman had not yet arrived; they began to worry. Did he get caught? Did he go to the city to turn the pages in? They huddled around in the cold abandoned building that was soon to become a Halfway's-house. All they could do was watch the dying solar powered clock on the wall and the doorless doorway, waiting for anything, even a shadow to appear. But, after long, they began to fear that even Rodman's shadow would be a no show in the shadowless city.

The Sun Comes to Freeman

The minutes felt like hours. The cold air was not helping any either. After another forty minutes, finally, Rodman came trudging down the hallway and into the hangout-turned-hideout. They all breathed a sigh of relief. "Where did you go?" they asked, "And what is that on your coat?" It was snow, but it was only early August; this was a problem. They began to tear apart what little furniture was left in the house in order to get wood to build a fire in the middle of the cement floor.

Once the fire got going and they could comfortably talk about what had just happened, Khalil stood there with them, confused. His friends, embarrassed for him but not because of him, asked, "What's really going on Lil'man?" Khalil told them how he rescued the woman after the earthquake and found the documents in the tunnel, not the North Hills as the media alert claimed. He told them there were no other books when he was down there, just the one. Then he told them how Mr. Screwtape got up suddenly and left once he found out about "The Book of Trumaine." As they stood trying to make sense of it all, each one of their connectors began buzzing. The city had the ability to send emergency messages to every connector, even when they were turned off. The boys retrieved the message and learned that later that evening, Mr. Shaman, Mr. Ivan Ben Ruind the 3rd and Mr. Screwtape would hold a press conference to discuss the meaning of the newfound pages.

The message also said that the boy who had stolen the missing pages had returned them to the city. Attached, was a very blurry video of a teen returning the documents, and also a very clear close-up of "The Book of Trumaine" being entered into the city's library reserve for rare and special books. Everyone turned and looked suspiciously at Rodman who had not yet given Khalil back his scroll. Rodman laughed, "How y'all gonna look at me like that? I don't know who that is but it ain't me." He pulled the rolled up pages from the small of his back. "I had to cover them up, from the snow. But all the pages you gave me are right here."

The group of friends laughed a relieved laugh. Daymen began trying to piece together the puzzling events. "This proves they were lying. Mr. Shaman is already about to explain the meaning but he just got the pages back. They have a 'Book of Trumaine' and so do we. So maybe there were two copies." Khalil chimed in, "Yeah, I found one and they must have had the other one stashed away for some reason." This puzzled Khalil even more. The young men decided that they should all meet back up to watch the press conference later that evening to try and pick up more clues. They were all excited. Not one of them was a junior city agent yet, and already they had their first case to solve.

In the meantime, Khalil wanted to take a trip to the West Hills to get some answers or, at least, to ask some questions. Dayman volunteered to join him. On their journey, the weather seemed to be getting colder by the hour. The sky was getting darker too. They traveled well into the afternoon and reached the foot of the West Hills around four o'clock. They had no energy to climb the hill but an older man who lived near the bottom spotted them and asked what they were looking for. After talking for a while, the old man asked Khalil, "What's your name boy?" He told him but the man rejected it saying, "No, your last name." "Freeman," he told him. The man hurried away but said, "Wait here."

Moments later, another old man came down from a little higher up the hill and began looking at Khalil intently. The first old man came back out and said, "Didn't I tell you?" "Tell him what?" Khalil asked. The second old man's eyes began to tear up as he shook his head, "You look so much like my brother Trumaine. Our last name is Freeman too, but he died over forty years ago and never had any children. I came to live here after the city killed him and broadcasted his body being thrown into Gehenna.

Khalil consoled the old man but did not tell him about the pages of the book he found with his brother's name on it. He and Dayman began to ask all sorts of questions. They found out that the N.I.N.T.E. was still very active; living in secrecy and making frequent trips into the city. Almost none of the living members had been up the great hill to see Newman, so there were very few Free-hands in the community. But they lived off of the aroma from old menus and the hope of Newman's return. The old man talked with them for nearly two hours until Dayman reminded Khalil that they had to get back to watch the press conference with the others. They thanked the old man for his time and then turned to leave.

But the old man called them back to give Khalil something; it was a menu. "I'm told it belonged to my brother," he said. The old man shook his head and then added, "You know, I never liked that Kakei. Never could see what my brother saw in her. But, she was nice enough to give me that menu after he died. I remember the first time Trumaine tried to share it with me," he laughed but did not finish his thought. Instead, he told Khalil, "I know it was really special to him and I think he'd want you to have it now."

At that point, Khalil realized that his grandmother had lied to him about not knowing Trumaine. But he could not focus on that because as he read over the menu, he experienced that same filling phenomenon that others had when they first peered into it. This rejuvenated the starving youngster, even while it made him all the more hungry for that which the menu advertised. He wondered out loud if what was happening to him was some kind of special reward that he earned by giving up on the city's fast food. But the old man told him, "I'm sure you're a little proud of yourself for making that sacrifice. But, remember, you came here starving and empty. There is nothing that you could have done to fill yourself back up; not like this. This is all Newman and the aroma from his menu." Immediately, Khalil offered the menu to Dayman who enjoyed the sensation as well. Then Khalil saw that what the old man said was true. The two young friends took note of the fact that, while they were looking into the menu, it suddenly felt like a true summer day.

The old man handed them a branch lit with fire. Pointing toward the city he said, "I ain't never seen the sky lookin' that dark. Use this to light your path. And if your fire starts going out, use the menu to fan the flame back up." The teens walked back talking about their strange experience. Particularly, how the old men didn't seem to be cold at all the entire time they were with them.

They made it back to the city just in time and met up with the others at Khalil's house. They gathered around the family's large connector. The media center had placed one in every home to keep people connected. Khalil's father didn't want to watch the press conference. "I don't' know why y'all wanna see that mess. All they're gonna do is lie to you," he complained. "Dad," Khalil said, "Do you even

know what's going on? They found documents from
forty-two years ago. I found documents from forty-
two years ago, first; right outside your job!" As he
was trying to persuade his father to care, the press
conference began.

Mr. Screwtape opened with, "Men and women
of Nameless City; we have made the most important
discovery of our life time. It seems that all this time,
we have been lied to. Not by the city or its
ambassadors from other regions, but by the
infamous 90. It turns out that Newman has not been
the enemy. His so-called "friends" outside the city
have been trying to get us to go up into the hills to
meet Newman, even though they knew there was a
risk that we could be attacked by lions and other
dangers along the way. We did not know this
information until now. We sent a lot of people up the
hill to work on the condos, and to restore the mall.
Many of them who have not come back were
probably ambushed by these so called 'friends' of
Newman. But, I was helped to see the light by my
wife's grandson. Some of you have seen the video
clips of him in the playgrounds speaking about
Newman earlier today. He pointed out that in those
old stories about me saving the city all those many
years ago, I was never really fighting against
Newman; it was the 90 who was the real enemy,
using Newman's name in vain to try to take over the

city. But tonight, we have some exciting news to tell you. For that, I will turn the floor over to Mr. Shaman."

Mr. Shaman got up and opened the book of the N.I.N.T.E. then said, "It appears that forty-two years ago, some of the members of the 90 decided to write and hide a secret book for us to find and read in the future. Maybe they didn't like the fact that their leaders were trying to keep Newman all to themselves instead of sharing him with the city. But, whatever the reason, we have found their book and we now know the secrets." Mr. Shaman turned to a section of the book that had been written by one of the N.I.N.T.E. members who had not been to the top of the great hill, to Newman's table. He began to read a passage that did not sound anything like what Khalil had read in "The Book of Trumaine." In fact, it directly contradicted it. The cameras zoomed in on the words as Shaman read. This was done for dramatic effect and to authenticate his words in the public's eye. Then, looking directly into the cameras, Mr. Shaman said, "And do you know what this means my friends? It means that Newman is not waiting for us on the hill tops as the 90 used to say. No! He is waiting for us, in Gehenna!"

Mr. Screwtape got back up at the podium and looked directly into the cameras to say, "I know my friends, this all sounds very strange. But there's something you need to know. Forty-two years ago, Newman appeared in the fires of Gehenna and had a meal with his true friends; a meal like you have never experienced before. Then he took them all with him to the underground mall. I'm going to turn it over to Mr. Conman from the media center at this point."

Mr. Conman got up and said, "When I first heard that Newman desired to dine with us in the fires of Gehenna, I didn't believe it. Surely, I thought, if this had ever happened before there would be video footage of it in the media center's file history. We keep a record of everything that anyone ever sends through their connector. So I dedicated over half of my staff to searching for any footage or media data concerning Newman, and sure enough, we found two data entries. The first proves that Trumaine was a real person who lived forty-two years ago. The following is an excerpt from an instant thought message sent by the same Trumaine who we believe is the author of the 90's secret book that bears that name:

Friends of Newman, we must STAND the HEAT. Jump with us, out of the city's frying pan and into the FIRE. If you make it, your New friends WOOD be NEAR waiting to receive you with free handed fellowship.

"Now, this sounds like a strange invitation, until you see the second data entry. What you are about to see is going to blow your mind." At that point, the media center broadcasted an edited version of the video footage taken down by Gehenna when Newman came to rescue and dine with his friends in the fire. They did not show anyone being forced into the flames. Nor did they show anyone suffering. They only showed Newman walking through the fire in slow-motion; next they showed Newman seated at the table dining with his friends; and then, Cartman jumping into the flames and finding a seat prepared for him. They also showed the two bystanders who tried to become participants, but the video stopped just before Newman turned to rebuke them with his eyes.

Mr. Screwtape returned to the podium and said, "We will now hear from the Media Review Board. As you know, the M.R.B. is an independent organization which exists to verify the authenticity of media content." A representative from the M.R.B. stood up and said, "We have verified that the footage was recorded approximately forty-two years ago and is indeed authentic. But we cannot determine to what extent it has been edited. Still, it is our professional opinion that no amount of editing can change the fact that someone walked through the fires of Gehenna and sat down to eat a meal with as many as fourteen other people. If we had the rest of the footage, we could tell you mo . . ." Mr. Screwtape stood back up and moved the microphone closer to his own mouth and said, "Thank you. Now, we will not be taking any questions because we don't have any answers. All we know is that, according to these secret books of the 90, and Trumaine's instant thought message, Newman does not show up until those who are looking for him have entered the fire first."

Just then, Mr. Shaman shouted out, "Wait a minute. Wait a minute. Now I understand the last secret book of the 90. Our extremely cold summer has been predicted. Newman knew that this wintery season was coming and has always planned to rescue us by calling us into Gehenna." The camera zoomed in on the page Shaman was reading and, sure enough, it did say that the end would be a time of extreme and bitter cold and that the sun would distance itself from the city because the city had distanced itself from the son. Mr. Shaman warned, "Some of you may have already realized that this secret book of the 90 can be found if you search for it in your connectors. But please, do not go trying to interpret it on your own. It is very confusing and you may do more harm than good. Just let us do the interpreting. That will cut down on the chaos." Most people honored this request. But some did not.

"It all makes sense," Mr. Screwtape said, sounding convincingly satisfied. "Men and women of Nameless City, I cannot tell you what to do, for I am only an ambassador from my region to yours. Any other title I have here is strictly honorary. But I would hope that you would meet us down by Gehenna to meet Newman there. If I had more power over your city though, I could do more to help you in this time of distress. I don't know how many people Newman can take to the underground mall, but in my region we have plenty of room underground to house people until things warm back up on the surface." Then, Mr. Ivan Ben Ruind the 3rd stood up and said, "My title is not honorary. So I *can* tell the city what to do. We are in a state of emergency and I can't have people staying and freezing to death in the city when we have a possible way out. City agents will be going throughout the city enforcing the new emergency plan; effective at midnight tonight, everyone is to meet down by Gehenna. We will all be saved by Newman tonight!"

After the press conference, messages began pouring in from the citizens of Nameless City, calling for an emergency vote that would give Mr. Screwtape executive power over the city. Iv'Ben organized a committee and within the hour, Mr. Screwtape was sworn in as the Supreme Head of Nameless City. But strangely, as soon as Screwtape took the oath, all of the city's power went out and all of the lights, off. None of the stars in the sky were close enough or bright enough to assist in illuminating the land as they normally did. The city was now darker than it had ever been before. After about five minutes the back-up power kicked in and some light returned. But, because the sun had been so distant for so long, none of the solar panels powering the reserve supply had much juice to give at all. This made the city all the more eerie now as the extreme darkness was only offset by what could only be described as very dark light.

Screwtape knew that it was too little too late. He got his executive power just as he had run out of time. All he could do now was hope that, once he got the people into Gehenna, his boss would be pleased. In the realm where Screwtape resided, his boss was not able to motivate employees by promising them any rewards, but only with the notion of inflicting on them less abuse. And so, he began thinking of ways to secure less agony for himself. He knew that his boss had different types of plans for using and destroying different types of people. So, he figured his boss would be pleased if he created an upper-class category, to be exploited separately from the general population of Nameless City. He pulled Ivan Ben Ruind the 3rd to the side and said to him discretely, "What if there was a way to take the best and the brightest of Nameless City to my region where accommodations of the highest sort could be made for a select few? I mean, if Newman is willing to entertain and put up with the mess of the masses, do we really want to be lumped in with them? I'm sure my boss can offer a more refined lifestyle for the city's elite class." Iv'Ben listened as they walked halfway down a dark hallway and continued their shady conversation.

Meanwhile, Khalil's friends sat silently in his dimly lit house, struggling to piece together the puzzling events. But Khalil had noticed something, two things actually that he couldn't stop thinking about. The first was in the video footage the media center had just broadcasted; and the second, was asleep on the couch beside him. "Dad," he shouted. His father shot up in his reclined chair. "What? What is it? Is it the city?" he yelled. The teens laughed, while trying hard to respect their elder. Khalil asked him, "How old are you dad?" His father responded, "Old enough that I don't have to answer to you," he laughed. "Seriously dad, I need to know. Aren't you turning forty-two next week?" His father shook his head and said, "Uh oh, I'm starting to look my age, hunh? So what?" But that was the least of Khalil's worries. He asked his father, "What ever happened to my real granddad—your father?" He put his head back down in his reclined chair and responded sadly, "He went up the great hill, and never came back down."

Khalil jumped up and ran out of the house. His friends tried hard to keep up as they looked for the failing light from his connector to follow his path. He ran to his grandmother's house and banged on the door. After a minute or two of standing in the cold, the door opened to him. His friends finally caught up and went inside with him. "Grandma' K, tell me the truth," he pleaded. "The truth? What truth?" she pretended to wonder. "You mean about Newman? You'll have to ask Mr. Screwtape about that." But Khalil would not let her off. "No. Not about Newman," he said. "Tell me about my real grandfather—Trumaine." Dayman thought back to the conversations they had earlier with Trumaine's brother and began making sense of it all.

Kakei's motion slowed almost to a pause. "What makes you think Trumaine was your grandfather?" she asked. "I have his last name," he answered. But she came back, "How do you know his last name? Besides, a lot of people have that last name." But he persisted, "I look like him." She turned, "How do you know what he looked like?" Khalil informed her, "I met his brother today, living in the West Hills. You gave him Trumaine's menu and he gave it to me. He said Trumaine's body was thrown into Gehenna but you told my dad that his father never came back from up the hill." But she still lied, "There, you see? One's up the hill, one's down in the fires; so they can't be the same person." Then Khalil insisted, "Stop lying Grandma' K. I saw you!" But she had no idea what he meant. Neither did his friends.

He continued, "They showed an old video of Newman sitting in the flames of Gehenna with some of his friends; just sitting there, eating and talking in the fire! But the person who recorded it didn't have a steady hand. He kept panning to the left. Halfway in the screen was a young woman; she looked just like you did forty-two years ago, except she had regular chains on her wrist. The woman was wearing the same outfit you're wearing in that digital picture over there of you and Mr. Screwtape, dated forty-one years ago. The only difference is, in the picture, you have fancier looking chains. But how is it that in that picture, and in the video down by Gehenna, you were not pregnant and yet my dad is turning forty-two next week?"

Khalil's friends marveled at his deductive skills. Dayman blurted out, "Dag Lil'man. You really should be a city agent." He looked at them, demanding silence. And then, Kakei began to cry. Amidst her tears, she forced out the words, "Every time I see you or your father, I'm reminded of the best thing I ever did—and the worst." "What are you talking about Grandma'?" he asked. She took her time, and then began to explain. "I didn't mean for anybody to get hurt. It just got away from me. I loved Trumaine with all my heart. We had history together, you know? We did a lot of things. We had our issues, but we were gonna work it out. But he went up that hill, and even though he came back, it was like . . . like he never really came back, you know? He didn't come back to me.

"Then, he met someone else. I didn't want anyone else to have him. So, right after he got married I had him arrested. I was only trying to make life hard for him and Angelique. But Screwtape, I guess he didn't like the fact that I still had feelings for Trumaine. Screwtape had me. He didn't want me, but he didn't want me to want anybody else. I think that's why he had Trumaine killed.

"After that, the city's agents kept Trumaine's wife and sister under supervision for three weeks, trying to get them to give up information about the N.I.N.T.E.'s plans. Screwtape found out that they were still alive and wanted to kill them both. But when he saw Angelique, somehow he instantly knew she was pregnant. He knew that he would never be able to give me a child. Underneath that coat he always wears, he's covered with countless chains all over, from his neck to his waist, to his wrists, to his feet, and he can never remove them. All these years, he's never even touched me. So he told me that I could keep Angelique's baby once it was born, but only the baby could live. Angelique would still have to be killed.

"I wanted to right the wrong that I had done to Trumaine. So I figured I would raise his child to replace the life that I took from him." Khalil cut her off, "What happen to Angelique? What happened to my grandmother?" Kakei cried all the more, but Khalil waited and then demanded the truth. She finally answered, "After your father was born, she nursed him for a little while. She became so attached to him. But one day, the city agents rushed in and snatched him from her. You know, I never taught him to hate city agents. I taught him not to trust them, but the hate . . . I think he got from that day. I think he still remembers. They separated him from his mother and before he made it out of the room, they ended her life."

Filled with anger and hurt, Khalil asked, "Why did you stay? Why would you stay with Mr. Screwtape all these years?" But her response struck his heart with a violent sadness. "He's gonna take me to the underground mall," she said with childlike naivety. Khalil got up and stormed towards the door. He couldn't leave fast enough. His friends had no words to console him. They only aimed to be near him in his hour of distress. Kakei followed them to the door and yelled, "Come to Gehenna with me. I bet Newman will reunite us with everyone we've lost. He'll make everything right. He'll give us all new things from the new mall." But Khalil ran harder to escape the sound of her voice.

He ran toward Gehenna, thinking that he would confront and, perhaps, kill Mr. Screwtape. Even if he was thrown into the fire, at least he will have stood up for his true family. It was too dark for him to run too fast. Dayman caught up with him and demanded to know what he planned to do. Khalil had no real plan. Rodman joined them and after listening to the confused emotions coming from his friend he advised, "Look, whatever we do, we can't stand here. We are going to freeze to death. My connector says it's going down to 3° tonight and it almost feels like it right now. If we get to Gehenna, I might jump in just to get warm." But Dayman had an idea, "Remember what happened when we read the menu earlier? We got warm didn't we?" Khalil nodded his shivering head. He pulled out the menu and shared its blessing with the others. All but one of them was able to enjoy its benefits. Then Dayman asked, "What do you wanna do Lil'man?" Khalil thought for a warm minute and then said, "I don't want to go to Gehenna. If all of the city agents are moving people to the south that means there's probably nobody guarding the great hill. We should head up the hill—to the top—to Newman!" They agreed. "One more thing," he said. "I don't want y'all to call me Lil'man no more. From now on, just call me Freeman." They agreed and took off heading toward the great hill. But one of them, the youngster who could not enjoy the benefit of the menu's blessing, turned from them and headed south, toward the flames.

Kakei arrived at Gehenna in style. She made her way through the crowd and went to stand by her husband who leaned over and whispered to her, "Today I'll make good on all my promises to take you to the underground mall." But Kakei, who always looked to get close to the man in the highest position, asked, "So, should I be thanking you, or just wait a little while and thank Newman?" Screwtape smiled with hate as he leaned over to Mr. Conman and Ivan Ben Ruind the 3rd to assure them, "As soon as we get these unprofitable souls into Gehenna, I'll lead our people up the hill to my region. My boss is waiting for us there with the keys to the underground. Newman can have these fools if he chooses to rescue them from their stupidity." The men smiled as they looked down on the people of Nameless City. Then Iv'Ben stepped up and announced to the crowd, "Beautiful people of Nameless city, tonight we will become a part of history. We will do what only few before us have done. We will do what our entertainers have only pretended to do for years. We will celebrate life in the flames of Gehenna and travel with Newman to the underground mall! Let the exodus from Nameless City begin!"

The crowds cheered but no one moved. Mr. Shaman leaned over to tell Screwtape and the others, "They want to see their leaders go into the flames first. You can't lead from behind." Screwtape responded, "I'm paying to you to be *their* spiritual adviser, not mine. Now do your job and get them to go in." But for all of Mr. Shaman's efforts, the crowd would not go into Gehenna. Then, Screwtape stood up and said, "Dear friends, we would go in before you, but we don't know how this all works or, if we'll be able to come back out once we've gone in. So we need to remain out here at first, just to make sure that everything goes smoothly." And yet, still, no one moved.

But Screwtape was not bothered by this in the least. He was a very patient man whose patience was about to pay off. He had been waiting years to do to Kakei what he planned to do ever since he first met her and became offended by her lie. He hated her from that day forward but had nonetheless posed for many happy pictures with her. He was always publically affectionate toward her so as to create the impression that he was madly in love with his wife. He did all that, just for a moment such as this. Holding the microphone to his mouth, he leaned over to put his arm around Kakei and said, "My dear, it appears that we are to be first into the flames."

Kakei waved to the crowd and the crowd cheered. Possessed with the thought of entering the mall, she turned to face the flames and said, "I'm waiting." Screwtape had never passed through the fire without experiencing extreme torment. He turned to Mr. Conman and said "Turn up the music." He did this to drown out the horrific sounds he was sure to make in the coming moments. Conman turned up the music and drained nearly all of the city's remaining power.

Then, Screwtape turned from the crowd and ushered his wife into the fires of Gehenna. He wrapped his coat around her, his long coat which was able to retard the flames only minimally. He screeched and screamed in a most inhuman way as he walked her all the way through to the back of the underground mall. She, too, screamed an inconsolable scream as she suffered from the scorching of sulfur at the very center of her soul. He left her on the other side of Gehenna, charred and smoldering as the flames refused to completely leave her flesh. Then, suddenly, a door open and someone or something from inside the mall grabbed Kakei and pulled her through. But she was in too much anguish to care or understand what was happening to her.

Still in pain himself, Screwtape received comfort only from the thought of Kakei suffering in the mall. Then, using his coat to cover his face, Mr. Screwtape let out a horrible scream as he forced himself back through the flames. He hated having to endure such pain and looked forward to watching the people of Nameless City suffer all the more now for costing him so much just to be able to fool them. When Mr. Conman saw Screwtape coming through the flames, his mouth dropped. He knew that the plan was to trick the masses into Gehenna but he had no idea how Screwtape was doing such a masterful job at making it look safe to enter. All his life, he lived to make the impossible look possible, and this was the epitome of that. The sixty-four year old Conman applauded him like an astonished child who had just seen the best show in the world.

Screwtape came out and grabbed the microphone and professed, "I saw him. I saw Newman! He received my wife. She's dining with him right now and you can too. But you have to pass all the way through. C'mon!" At his words, those in the front of the crowd were pushed further forward by those in the rear who desired to go in but wanted more proof that it was safe. Then the running began. Some ran to get to the mall; some, to get to the food at Newman's table; and others, just to get out of the way of the charging mob. Those who entered but wanted to turn back could not because so many others were filing in right behind them.

Many who entered were snatched up by the wicked ex-employees of Newman and his father who roamed the underground mall. Others writhed as they suffered severely in the flames of the great fire which burns continually. As the thousands in the crowd waited impatiently, pushing their way toward the heat, Screwtape and a few hundred men and women began traveling in the cold toward the great hill. Along with the city's "elite," he also brought a large number of city agents, thinking that perhaps, they could be fed to Curse and Consequence while his boss decided what to do with the others.

Further north, Khalil Freeman and his friends had gotten beyond the food court at the end of Straight Street and made it to the Chain Exchange gate, but no one was there. Freeman, as he was now called, remembered reading in "The Book of

Trumaine" how he had to have his chains removed in order to be permitted to travel up the hill. Then he said, "Everyone, look at your hands. Do you see anything?" They began to laugh until they looked and saw the images of the lions on their hands. "Those lions represent Curse and Consequence. The heavy chain on your right hand shows that you are tied to a curse. The links chained to your left hand mark the years you may live, filled with the consequences of disregarding Newman and his father's health code; you can count them if you want, but no one has more than 120 links. There are two lions up ahead and a very crafty individual who manipulates their chains. He will seek to deceive us and the lions will seek to devour us. But you must look to Newman. He rescues travelers from the lions. Do y'all believe this?" he asked. And they did.

Just then, the ground began to move behind them. It was not a quake; only small plots of earth were moving. They looked with puzzled faces until a small hole in the ground opened up and people began coming out one by one. Then another whole opened up several feet away. And more people began popping up from beneath the surface. They identified themselves as members of the N.I.N.T.E. and told how they had been going down to Gehenna to convince people that Newman would not meet them there. Those who listened were led back through the tunnels to the great hill. The members of the N.I.N.T.E. rescue party were shocked to find that the great hill seemed just as cold and dark as the city. Some of the men and women rescued from Gehenna turned to go back down to the food court to eat. They would not travel up the hill since many of them had not eaten in quite a while due to the closing of a large number of Halfway's-houses in the city.

The rest of the group began traveling together toward the top; to the place where none of them had ever been before. But they knew to continue straight up, just as the Chain Exchange guard would have directed them. As they went further, the bitter cold and thick blackness of the night made climbing the hill a most difficult and dangerous feat. At several points, members of their pack began to give up and had to be convinced by the others to carry on. Almost all of them thought that they would freeze or starve to death at some point in the journey.

It was not long before they began to see, towards the top of the hill, a bright light shining. But they were still a long ways from it. As they looked back behind them, they could barely see, but were eventually able to make out two more groups of people following them further down the hill. "It's more N.I.N.T.E., with men and women rescued from

Gehenna," one of them said. They continued climbing but did not notice that the light at the top of the hill was getting brighter and closer. After a while, however, they did notice that they were no longer rubbing themselves to keep warm. Dayman looked back down the hill and noticed that the group which was furthest away was starting to look more like an army than a rescue party. He told Freeman who agreed that they were being trailed by city agents. He panicked and shouted to those traveling with him, "We've gotta run!"

Freeman remembered, at that point, how "The Book of Trumaine" mentioned getting lighter and almost floating to the top as one traveled higher up the hill. He looked at the ground to see if he was still in contact with it and saw that he was. But to his surprise, he saw his shadow being projected behind him. This thrilled and frightened him. The sun was returning! They would not freeze to death. But at the same time, he wondered, "Are we running into the sun? Is that even possible?" Looking again towards the hilltop, he noticed the light getting even closer and brighter, but he was still able to look directly into it. He figured they had two choices: either run to the fires of Gehenna below or run to the sun shining above. He had made his choice. Forgetting about those traveling with him, Freeman took off and ran even harder to get even higher.

After a while, he came to the halfway point on the hill and stopped when he saw the SOUL FOOLED restaurant sitting off on the side of the road. He figured that since he had outrun his friends, maybe he could stop and just have a look around while he caught his breath and waited for them to catch up. Curse and Consequence were crouched there as they had always been. But the lions were hard to notice because as he looked, Freeman saw all kinds of precious stones and shining ornaments sitting on the top step, seeming as if they had been placed there specifically for him. He knew from reading Trumaine's book that this was a dangerous place to be, but he also began to think about the many ways his life would be different if he possessed the treasures sitting before him. Most importantly, he could finally get the respect he craved. No one would ever dis him because of his height again. And, he could take pride in the fact that he did not have to go through Gehenna to get any of it.

The owner of that false food establishment came to the door and called to him, "This is where you wanna be. You've tasted my food in the city but it's nothing like my food here on the hill. Did you know that the entrance to the mall is located behind me? And it's not abandoned as you've been told. All the things you see sitting here in front of me are from the mall. They're mine and I can give them to you if you come in and dine with me." The owner opened the door and said, "That's not all. There's someone here who's been waiting to meet you. Isn't that right?"

At that point, a man came from behind the owner, looking like a much older version of Freeman. The man smiled a very believable smile and said, "You've done a great job son. You followed all the clues and you found me. Your father was right. I never came back down the hill. I've been up here this whole time. I know it seems wrong but, once you come in, you'll see why I stayed. But I'm so proud of you. You figured it all out on your own. You were smarter, stronger and faster than all of your friends. Ain't no need for you to endure all the way to the hilltop. You beat everybody to the halfway point and that's good enough for me. Now, I know you're starving, come and have a meal with your granddad."

By that time, the rest of the group began to approach the halfway point. They looked and saw Freeman walking slowly down the pathway toward the door. But when each one of them looked at the entrance, they saw only their greatest desire sitting in front of the door, waiting for them to come and claim it. Everyone was then tempted by the owner to enter into SOUL FOOLED. Some began to take steps toward the path, not even noticing Curse and Consequence who had stood up and began moving toward them.

But Rodman, who still held Freeman's menu, was not interested in whatever was there for him. He opened the menu and noticed immediately that it was most certainly not from the place that stood before them. He got in front of Freeman and Dayman to push them back and would not let them pass. He forced them to look at the menu, pointing out the differences between what was written in it and what was being offered at SOUL FOOLED. "Look how dark that place is. It's only a few yards away and it looks like the blackest night, even darker than the city. And it smells like Gehenna."

Then, Dayman snapped out of the strong spell he seemed to be under and said, "Dag, you're right. Why is it so dark? We need to get back out onto the road, into the broad day light." Freeman too snapped back to his senses, embarrassed by the fact that he had been deceived and led off the path, and, also by the fact that he was likely the cause of the others getting off track. He began backing away from SOUL FOOLED. "I guess it doesn't really matter if I'm the fastest or the strongest," he thought to himself, putting much less confidence in his flesh. He called out to those who had gone further in, "It's a trap.

Don't go!" But they were entranced and only continued moving forward.

Just then, a gust of wind came rushing down the hill and remained in the air. The aroma it carried was so powerfully pleasant that it broke the strong hold that was on the travelers and began luring them back to the road. The owner of that cursed café shouted, "Links!" Inside the restaurant, his employee, the one who made himself to look like Freeman's grandfather, added as many links as he could to the chains of Curse and Consequence. The lions took off running full speed after their prey and without much effort even, got close enough to strike. They jumped into the air with every intention of landing on and crushing and then devouring Newman's future friends.

But suddenly, a flash of the most brilliant light traveled across the entire vicinity and lingered in the air like lightning-in-slow-motion. The light forced Curse and Consequence to the ground, hurting their pride. It was undeniable that, at that moment, something authentically different was happening. It felt like the instant daybreak of a new and unending day. Freeman looked down and saw that the shadow beneath his feet was gone again; but this time, it was not for lack of light, but because of the presence of it. There was so much ambient sunshine that there was no place for a shadow to exist; no room for darkness at all.

Freeman also noticed that now, he was floating. Now, the air was sweet like he had read about in "The Book of Trumaine." Now, there was a very present joy in what he and his friends inhaled which produced laugher in response to every breath. They looked and saw the owner of the SOUL FOOLED restaurant cower back inside and run away from the door. The restaurant itself could not withstand the intensity of the light. It broke apart and disintegrated. Curse and Consequence took off running down the hill. They kept running past the other pack of N.I.N.T.E members until they came upon Mr. Screwtape and his entourage. Upon seeing their chains, the lions began viciously attacking them.

Mr. Screwtape narrowly escaped the attack. He did not initially plan to travel up the hill with the city's elite. He knew that there was a strict "no chains" policy on the hill and that his could not be removed by the guard who sat there. He planned only to lead his entourage to the Chain Exchange gate. After which point, he himself would turn back to go enter the mall through Gehenna and meet up with them again when they reached the entrance halfway up the hill. But when he saw that no one was guarding the Chain Exchange gate, he decided to accompany them. That is, until Curse and Consequence cancelled that plan and sent him running back down into the city, toward Gehenna.

Further up the hill, Freeman was captivated the new phenomenon occurring. He looked intently into the light which descended up him. He was certain that he was looking into the sun but was confused as to why he had not been burned or blinded; he was not even straining to see. Then, from within the center of the light source, a man appeared, and with him, a countless number of souls looking more content than Freeman had ever seen anyone look.

Based on what he had read in Trumaine's book, Freeman was sure that the one in the center of the crowd was Newman, accept he did not look anything like the weak pictures people had drawn of Newman in the playgrounds, nor did he look quite the way Trumaine described him. Instead, he was positively radiant. He did, however, still have the scars that Trumaine wrote about. But the scars appeared to be totally healed. Seeing that Freeman was staring at his wounds, the one in the center of the crowd invited him, "Go ahead, touch and see for yourself." Then, Freeman put his hand to one of the scars and felt the bruised flesh of the one giving him light. But, with a little pressure, the flesh gave way and a ray of light came beaming out of him. Freeman quickly pulled his hand away, not sure if he had done something wrong.

But the one shining upon him shifted his attention; he smiled and said, "Where are your chains?" Freeman and all those who were with him looked down and with amazement answered, "I don't have them anymore." The one holding the contented crowd together said, "And I will not chain you, but will only bind your heart to mine, if you are willing?" At that, Freeman and his friends each thought of the perilous drama unfolding in the city and imagined how much more pleasant their history and their future would be if this glowing gentleman were a present friend. They replied, "We are willing." Instantly, each one of them was clothed with colorful bands of energy and light. They looked down at their new raiment and noticed that they no longer had any images of lions on their hands. "Come with me," the one in the center said, "We have a feast to attend."

They tried to walk down the hill with their halogen hero but their feet could not touch the ground. They traveled in what seemed like no time at all, and yet, they enjoyed themselves for quite a long while as they descended the hill. As they reached the bottom, they began to see the most unsightly scenes as the light which led them suddenly appeared to others and surprised the citizens of the Nameless City. The city was almost completely pitch-black. The only light within it was that which came from Gehenna. Under that dismal darkness all kinds of wickedness was being worked out on the city's streets.

Once men and women saw that Newman was not rescuing people from the great fire, their hate for him returned and was now even greater than it had been before. They ran from Gehenna but the wicked ex-employees from the mall chased many of them through the woods and mistreated them. Those who escaped the woods and made it back to the city were suddenly presented with opportunities to act out their own wickedness since the city was now dark and no one could see their deeds. On every street, people were assaulting and abusing one another in the most inhumane ways. Blood, tears and every other bodily fluid stained the ground of the city.

As Newman and his new friends made their way through the city, he brought with him his great light which frightened many. But aside from causing fear, there was such a great degree of difference between the quantity of darkness in the city and the quality of light coming from Newman that, many people ran back towards Gehenna to protect their eyes from the pain of peering upon his purity; or, to escape the pain of having his pure eyes peer upon them.

Newman opened his mouth and loudly pronounced a strange word. It was only one word but it seemed to have two very different effects upon those who heard it, so that some responded as if he said to them "Go," and they ran faster toward Gehenna; but others responded as if they heard him say, "Come," and those came out from their hiding places to have private conversations with Newman. Many of them were men and women who did not listen when Mr. Shaman told the citizens of Nameless City not to search for or read the N.I.N.E.T.E.'s digital book. Some of these joined the growing number of Newman's new community, but others did not.

From time to time, great flashes of light emanated from Newman. This light consumed any who came to protest his entrance into the city. And there were many who did so. But it seemed as if the light did more than consume would-be enemies. It demolished the city completely. It scorched and cleansed by fire everything that was built without considering Newman and his father's health-code— which was everything. Those who were walking with the luminescent leader began to cry as they saw their favorite landmarks, which triggered memories, being demolished. They cried all the more when they saw that Gehenna was still burning and remembered that many of their loved ones had gone into it.

But the living light in the center of the crying crowd said, "From the time my father began to invite your ancestors to come and dine with us, there have always been those who would reject his invitation. You might rejoice then in knowing that my father has prepared a place at his table for you, and bound his heart to you so that you would bind your hearts to mine and thereby, receive his invitation."

Then he sent out a pulse of energy that shook the city violently and caused it to quake at both ends. The great hill began to crumble so that instead of going up it now slanted down just as deep as it once went high. Then Gehenna, along with the mall, were ripped and lifted from their foundations and transported over to the once great hill which now descended into a great pit. There, they were let go as they dropped to the very bottom of that pit. A large, long, heavy chain, consisting of 1000 links appeared and flung itself through the air until it anchored itself, at one end, deep into the bedrock at the bottom of the great pit; and at the other end, around the neck of the ex-owner of that evil eatery which once deceived many.

Upon finding himself so shackled in that pit, the builder of SOUL FOOLED looked around to see if the lions which once guarded him were with him in Gehenna. When he saw that they were not, he immediately began trying to free himself of the restraint but he could not. He knew that if Curse and Consequence were still roaming around up above that it was not over for him just yet. And so, he began the long, arduous task of climbing the hill, determined to make one last attack on his hilltop enemy. The ex-owner of that ex-establishment was filled with even more evil rage because, even though his exalted enemy, Newman, had now taken up residence down in the city, his ex-employer was nonetheless still exalted very high above him as he struggled to free himself from his lowly pit.

Meanwhile, the one who was now lighting the city with himself had arranged for an astronomically large and yet extraordinarily intimate banquet table to be prepared for him and his countless guests. He had waited so long to sit and dine with each and every one of them. Finally, they sat together. As they ate, he talked with each one personally and with them all corporately. People reunited with loved ones who had been to the top of the great hill and rejoiced to see them again. Freeman met Tru-man and Angelique and Jermaine and Imani. But every conversation kept coming back to the benevolent beaming body of light at the head of the table.

All around them, there appeared a brand new mall filled with many good things. Everyone saw it, but no one seemed concerned with it. It was hard to pull oneself away from the table. Uman, who was there with his wife Evelyn, stood and asked his radiant rescuer, "So, should we call you Newman now? It's been such a long time, but I remember there was another name we called you before you came back to rescue us. And I think that name would be fitting." The others at the table asked what the name was; they desperately wanted to know all they could about the city's new sun and savior. Uman answered them, "We used to call him E-man. It was short for Immanuel, which means 'the living menu' or 'the menu lives with us'." They all agreed that not only was the name fitting for him as their new fuel and personal solar power, but that the city itself needed a new name, and there was none better for it.

The grateful guests around the table had many questions. Such as, who or what was it that came from the menus to satisfy their appetites? And why did the satisfaction only make them hunger for more? Was the breeze and aroma in the air now the same as that which radiated from the hilltop before? And why was it that they were all hearing Newman's father answer him when he spoke to him, but they had still not yet met him?

Periodically, different people would arise and go to work on a project assigned to them to help rebuild the city; such as changing the signs from Nameless City in order to reflect its new title. Curse and Consequence were not seen often, if at all. In fact, it was rumored that Curse had attacked and swallowed up Consequence and, as a result, had nearly doubled in size. But it would be a long time before the lion would make an appearance in Immanuel City. To be certain, though, he eventually did. And so did the builder of that dilapidated delicatessen who, for the time being, resided at the bottom of the great pit. And when they did, all of Newman's answers to his guests' many questions finally made sense. But that is a story for another book, and another time. This book was merely the amazing story of how the son came to free man.

"Come, everyone who thirsts, come to the waters; and he who has no money, come, buy wine and milk without price. Why do you spend your money for that which is not bread and your labor for that which does not satisfy? Listen diligently to me, and eat what is good and delight yourselves in rich food. Incline your ear and come to me; hear, that your soul may live . . ."

-God (Isaiah 55:1-3)

10651145R00144

Made in the USA
Charleston, SC
20 December 2011